The Power of Poppy Pendle

By Natasha Lowe

A PAULA WISEMAN BOOK

Simon & Schuster Books for Young Readers

NEW YORK   LONDON   TORONTO   SYDNEY   NEW DELHI

SIMON & SCHUSTER BOOKS FOR YOUNG READERS

An imprint of Simon & Schuster Children's Publishing Division
1230 Avenue of the Americas, New York, New York 10020
This book is a work of fiction. Any references to historical events, real people, or real places are used fictitiously. Other names, characters, places, and events are products of the author's imagination, and any resemblance to actual events or places or persons, living or dead, is entirely coincidental.
Text copyright © 2012 by Natasha Lowe
Cover illustration copyright © 2012 by Seb Mesnard
All rights reserved, including the right of reproduction in whole or in part in any form.
Simon & Schuster Books for Young Readers is a trademark of Simon & Schuster, Inc.
For information about special discounts for bulk purchases, please contact Simon & Schuster Special Sales at 1-866-506-1949 or business@simonandschuster.com.
The Simon & Schuster Speakers Bureau can bring authors to your live event.
For more information or to book an event, contact the Simon & Schuster Speakers Bureau at 1-866-248-3049 or visit our website at www.simonspeakers.com.
Also available in a Simon & Schuster Books for Young Readers hardcover edition
Design by Chloë Foglia
The text for this book is set in Cochin.
Manufactured in the United States of America
0314 OFF
First Simon & Schuster Books for Young Readers paperback edition September 2013
4 6 8 10 9 7 5 3
The Library of Congress has cataloged the hardcover edition as follows:
Lowe, Natasha.
The power of Poppy Pendle / Natasha Lowe. — 1st ed.
p. cm.
"A Paula Wiseman Book."
Summary: Ten-year-old Poppy will do anything to realize her dream of becoming a baker, although her parents insist she attend Ruthersfield, the exclusive girls school for witchcraft, where she excels despite her dislike of magic. Includes baking tips and recipes.
ISBN 978-1-4424-4679-3 (hardback)
[1. Self-realization—Fiction. 2. Bakers and bakeries—Fiction. 3. Magic—Fiction. 4. Family life—Fiction. 5. Witches—Fiction. 6. Schools—Fiction.] I. Title.
PZ7.L9627Pow 2012
[Fic]—dc23
2012006735
ISBN 978-1-4424-4926-8 (pbk)
ISBN 978-1-4424-4680-9 (eBook)

For my parents—who have always believed in me and encouraged me to follow my passions. Kibet fallow da.

Chapter One

························

Poppy

POPPY PENDLE WAS BORN ON THE FLOOR OF A BAKERY, Patisserie Marie Claire, the fancy French bakery in the little town of Potts Bottom. Now, people don't usually give birth on bakery floors in the middle of a Thursday afternoon, but Edith Pendle did just that. She had no choice, even though her baby wasn't due for another two weeks. Poppy pushed her way out with the speed of an express train and was immediately wrapped up in a cake-scented tea towel by the kind lady who ran the shop. The customers cheered, and someone handed Edith Pendle a bag of little warm almond cakes. Sitting up in her mother's arms, Poppy breathed in deeply and reached for the bag of cakes. Then she did something quite unexpected. She gobbled them all down, waved her sugary fingers at the crowd, smiled, and gave a contented burp.

Although the Pendles didn't approve of giving birth in a bakery, no one could deny that their daughter was an amazing and extremely unusual child. By three months old, she had learned to walk, and could carry bags of shopping up Pudding Lane to the Pendles' little brick house. At the post office she usually caused quite a stir, leaping up and posting all the out-of-town mail through the top letter slot. "She's really advanced!" Roger Pendle liked to brag to their neighbors.

One late autumn day something happened that made Poppy's already proud parents even prouder. Mrs. Pendle's sister, Vivian, had come for a visit, and it was such a pleasant afternoon that the Pendles decided to have tea in the garden. Poppy had carried out her high chair and was settled next to Auntie Viv when her mother came parading across the lawn bearing a strange, pink-tinted cake on a tray.

"I've made an orange cake," Edith Pendle announced, which was a surprise in itself because she hardly ever cooked. "I got the recipe from the back of a can of tinned salmon. Apparently it's full of protein." Auntie Viv covered her mouth in horror and Poppy gagged, kicking her feet in the air. Poor Edith Pendle abruptly stumbled forward, as if she'd been pushed from behind, and dropped the cake on the grass with a splat.

"Oh dear!" Mr. Pendle said, a hint of relief in his voice.

"My cake!" Mrs. Pendle wailed while Poppy babbled away in her own private language. She waved her drooly fingers about, and a gorgeous chocolate cake covered in pink sugar roses suddenly appeared on the table.

"Now, where in heaven did that come from?" Auntie Viv gasped. Poppy chuckled and sucked on her toes, blowing pale pink bubbles into the air. As they popped, showers of sugared almonds scattered down.

"It's Poppy!" Mr. Pendle cried, staring at his daughter in disbelief. "She's got the gift, Edith. She's really got the gift. I don't believe it!" Poppy was clapping her hands together, and little chocolate doves were flying out of them. Mr. Pendle plucked one up and popped it into his mouth. "Oh, fantastic, Edith! Our Poppy's magic!"

Mr. Pendle worked in a shoe shop called Happy Feet, selling shoes to the people of Potts Bottom. It was boring, smelly work, being surrounded by cheesy feet all day long, and he certainly didn't want his daughter following in his footsteps. Now they could stop worrying, because Poppy was destined for much bigger things. Crouching beside her, he stuck his face close to Poppy's. "Who's a clever girl, then? Who's going to be a witch when she grows up?"

"I'm putting her name down for Ruthersfield Academy, first thing Monday morning!" Mrs. Pendle declared. "There hasn't been a witch in the family for three generations, not since Granny Mabel! I'm just tickled pink, I'm so proud. I do wish Poppy hadn't been born in a bakery though." She sighed. "It doesn't seem fitting, somehow."

Poppy made a loud noise like a raspberry, and a tiny gray cloud formed and hovered about twelve inches above the tea table. "Oh, look, she's at it again!" Mr. Pendle exclaimed. The Pendles watched in excitement as the storm cloud erupted, pouring water down onto the chocolate cake. Then Poppy scrunched up her face, turned the color of an overripe tomato, and burst into tears.

Straight after breakfast on Monday the Pendles telephoned Ms. Lavinia Roach, the headmistress at Ruthersfield Academy. Ms. Roach had never heard of a baby performing magic before. "This is really quite astonishing if what you are telling me is true," she told Edith Pendle. "But before I put Poppy down on our waiting list, I would appreciate seeing the child for myself. Sometimes parents go to rather extreme lengths to get their girls into Ruthersfield. We are, as I'm sure you well know, Mrs. Pendle, the only accredited school for magic in the country. And we are very selective."

"Oh, just wait till you see our little Poppy," Mrs. Pendle said. "I'm sure you'll be suitably impressed!"

So the next afternoon Poppy was promptly brought over to Ruthersfield for her interview. As the Pendles were ushered into the headmistress's office, Poppy kept trying to climb out of her carriage and trot back toward the door. "No, sweetheart," Edith Pendle insisted, grasping her daughter by the hand so she couldn't escape.

"Looks like she has other plans," Ms. Roach said, smiling down at Poppy.

"Well, she doesn't understand what an honor it is to be here," Edith Pendle said, tugging her daughter into the room. "This is quite an occasion for the Pendle family."

"I brought this with me," Poppy's father began, carefully extracting a sheet of white paper from a cardboard tube and unrolling it across Ms. Roach's desk. "Our family tree," he announced, bursting with pride and pointing a finger at the chart. "Well, my wife's family tree really. That's Great-Granny Mabel right there," he said, tapping at the paper, "but I'm sure you know all about her."

"Indeed!" Ms. Roach lowered her head in reverence. "What an honor for you all, being related to Mabel Ratcliff. One of the best head girls Ruthersfield ever had."

"And look," Roger Pendle said, breathing heavily over the chart. "Her great-great-great grandmother Irene had the gift as well, you see, so it runs in the family. We can go right back to the thirteenth century."

"Certainly quite remarkable, Mr. Pendle. Now, please, won't you all sit down?" Ms. Roach suggested. "I'll ring for some tea and biscuits." Poppy immediately climbed up into one of the chairs facing Ms. Roach's desk, and started to suck on her fingers. "While we wait, why don't you show me what sort of magic little Poppy can do?"

"Right then, come on, sweetheart," Mrs. Pendle said, tickling her daughter under the chin. "Show this nice lady your tricks." Poppy blew a raspberry, but nothing happened.

"Make some chocolate birdies appear," her father encouraged. Poppy paid no attention, and it was only when the school secretary brought in a tea tray that she began to get excited.

"Is Poppy allowed a biscuit?" Ms. Roach said, offering round a plate of chocolate shortbread. "We have a wonderful chef here at Ruthersfield. Everything's homemade." Poppy gurgled, bouncing up and down in her chair. Little marshmallow balls started to burst out of her lap and onto the desk, like popcorn exploding from a popcorn maker. One of them landed right in Ms. Roach's cup of tea.

"Now that's my clever girl," Mrs. Pendle said, planting a kiss on Poppy's forehead. The soft, sticky balls were bouncing about all over the room, but Poppy ignored them, munching away on a biscuit. When she had finished, she licked her fingers, gave a satisfied sigh, and blew out hundreds of tiny gold stars.

"Quite the show, eh!" Mr. Pendle said, brushing bits of stardust off his suit.

"Unbelievable!" Lavinia Roach agreed. "I have never seen anything like it. Your daughter is extraordinary. Ruthersfield Academy would be honored to offer her a place. She is far too young now, of course, but when she's seven we will be expecting her." Poppy scrunched up her face and blew a loud, windy raspberry. Pink, berry-shaped bubbles floated into the air, and when they popped, an overpowering stench of rotting fruit filled the room. Ms. Roach gave a nervous laugh. "It's a good thing your daughter's only six months old," she remarked. "Otherwise, I might think she didn't want to come to Ruthersfield Academy at all."

The older she got, the more apparent it became that it was cakes Poppy wanted to make and not spells. Around her fifth birthday she discovered a cookbook, *The Art of Simple Baking*, lodged under the fridge and covered in dust. It had been a wedding present to the Pendles and was still in its cellophane wrapping. Poppy dug the book out and spent most of her free time studying the photographs of tarts and cakes and rich butter cookies. At first her parents hadn't minded, because it kept her from staring longingly out the window, waiting for the school bus to drive by. If Poppy had had her way, she'd be going to the local elementary school with all the other kids in Potts Bottom. But Mr. and Mrs. Pendle refused to send her.

"Apparently, seven is the ideal age to begin learning for a witch," Edith Pendle told Poppy. "They have different methods up at the academy, and I don't want to interfere with them, sweetheart. Anyway, I'm not sure I want you mixing with nonmagic children," she had said. "You're special, Poppy." And Poppy certainly seemed to be. She had managed to teach herself to read, just so she could try out the recipes printed in the *Potts Bottom Gazette*.

"All Poppy ever does is bake." Edith Pendle said, fretting to her best friend, Maxine Gibbons, one spring afternoon. Maxine lived next door, and they were talking across the backyard fence while Poppy lay on the grass, reading her newest edition of *Good Eats* magazine. She had bought herself a subscription with her birthday money when she turned six and loved to pore over the pictures. "I don't know where she gets it from, I really don't. Certainly not me." Edith gave a nervous laugh. "What's wrong with a nice box mix, might I ask?"

Maxine giggled. "Well, she was born in a French bakery."

"Yes, but we don't mention that in front of her," Edith Pendle said, lowering her voice. "Honestly, Maxine, that is not something Poppy needs to know about. She'd want to buy bread there, or find out how they make those fancy cakes." Mrs. Pendle studied her daughter longingly. "I just don't understand it. I really don't." She shook her head and sighed. "What Poppy should be doing is concentrating on her magic."

"So when is her first day at Ruthersfield?" Maxine Gibbons asked.

"Not till September, but I'm so excited, Maxine! You should see the uniform, deep purple with gold trim. Poppy's going to look so smart."

"She doesn't seem very enthusiastic, does she?" Maxine said.

"No." Poppy's mother frowned. "Thank goodness she won't have time for this ridiculous cooking nonsense when she starts school."

Maxine shrieked with laughter and called over to Poppy. "You need to get cooking up some spells, my girl. Witches don't make cakes; they make magic."

"But I don't want to be a witch," Poppy whispered, wondering if there was something wrong with her. She wished she could stop herself from turning seven. Unfortunately, she knew that sort of magic was impossible for her, and in a few months' time, whether she liked it or not, she was going to be starting at Ruthersfield.

Chapter Two

· ·

No Time to Bake

THE NEXT THREE YEARS WERE MISERABLE ONES FOR POPPY. She hated everything about Ruthersfield Academy. Her life revolved around magic, and with all the homework she was expected to do, Poppy had almost no time left over for the thing she really loved, cooking. She would tiptoe downstairs extra early most days, just so she could still bake. "You cannot go off to school looking like this," Edith Pendle grumbled one morning, wiping at a butter stain on Poppy's uniform. "I mean, honestly, Poppy, you're almost ten years old and you still can't keep yourself clean."

"Oh, but, Mum, don't those look good?" Poppy

said, staring at a glossy picture of coconut cupcakes. "I had to try to make them." Her May issue of *Good Eats* magazine lay open on the counter, covered in blobs of raw batter.

Mrs. Pendle gave an exasperated sigh. "If you insist on getting up at the crack of dawn and mucking about in the kitchen, PLEASE WEAR AN APRON!"

"I'm sorry, Mum. I forgot."

"What I'd like to know is, how come you never forget when we run out of flour or sugar, or to reorder that cooking magazine of yours?"

"I'm honestly not sure," Poppy replied, as a blob of buttercream landed on her skirt.

"Well, in case you've FORGOTTEN, it's the Step-Up Ceremony next week, Poppy, and you'll become an Intermediate Witch. That means you're going to have to start to focus on your work more." Poppy's stomach flipped over. She hated thinking about the Step-Up Ceremony. It was an event anticipated with much excitement by most of the fourth formers, because they would now be old enough to take flying lessons. Poppy had no desire to "Step Up." School was awful enough as it was without having to worry about climbing onto a broomstick.

"Oh, Mum, that reminds me," Poppy said, sniffing the air and pulling a tray of cupcakes from the oven.

"Can you sign my report card, please? It's in the side pocket of my backpack, and I've got to take it back to school today."

"Your report card! Come on, Poppy! Why on earth didn't you give it to me last night?" Mrs. Pendle crouched down by the table and rummaged around in Poppy's backpack. It was slumped on the floor, and she huffed in annoyance as she pulled out a long, crumpled envelope. "These things do matter."

"I'm really sorry, Mum."

"I know, I know, you just forgot. Oh my goodness though, will you look at this!" Poppy's mother clapped a hand over her mouth. "Six As and two Bs. B in spell chanting and B in chemistry."

"I can't sing, Mum. That's why Miss Robinson gave me a B for spell chanting."

"And what about this B for chemistry?" Mrs. Pendle glanced at her daughter.

"Mum, I hate chemistry. It's my worst subject."

"Isn't it rather like cooking? You're good at that, Poppy, mixing ingredients together." And then unable to stop herself, she added, "If you put as much time into chemistry as you do baking, you'd be making the honor roll."

"But I love to cook," Poppy said softly, "and I really don't like making spells."

Mrs. Pendle ignored this. "Still, considering all your classes are advanced, you've done very well. I think this calls for a treat!"

"Really, Mum? Thanks! There's a new book on cake decorating that sounds great. Could I have that?"

Mrs. Pendle did not reply. Instead, she called out, "Six As, Roger!" waving Poppy's report card at her husband, who had just walked into the kitchen.

"Well done, love! That's fantastic!" Roger Pendle smiled at Poppy. "Although it doesn't surprise me one bit. You're as smart as your great-granny Mabel."

"Oh, I know what we should do to celebrate. We should take Poppy to the Museum of Magical Discoveries," Edith suggested. "That would make a lovely treat, wouldn't it?"

"If you don't mind, I'd rather have the cookbook," Poppy said, but Edith Pendle was already hurrying out the back door, clutching Poppy's report card. She couldn't wait to show it to Maxine.

It wasn't that Poppy tried particularly hard to do well at school, but magic just happened to be something she was extraordinarily good at. Even when her mind drifted in class, which it tended to do rather often, she was usually able to keep up. In math they were learning how to divide large quantities of spell ingredients and add different potions together to make a spell balance correctly. Geography was all about studying the best places in the world to practice magic. "Location, location, location," Miss Higgle, their geography teacher, was constantly telling the fourth formers. You didn't want to practice magic in the desert: too hot, not enough water, and it was almost impossible to keep your ingredients from drying out. Hilly areas were fine, but mountainous regions like the Swiss Alps were terrible. Spells ricocheted about off the rocky walls and ended up in all the wrong places. Not that Poppy had the slightest interest in any of these things, but she did try to pay attention, even when she was thinking about new cookie recipes.

The day before the Step-Up Ceremony, Poppy celebrated her tenth birthday. She had invited Megan Roberts, Fanny Freeman, and some of the other girls in her class to a party, but apparently none of them could come, which didn't surprise Poppy one bit. She had only invited them to please her mother. These girls weren't real friends. Not the sort of friends you could laugh and share secrets with. In fact, most of them teased Poppy because she liked to read cooking magazines, and sometimes called her "cake head," since her hair always smelled of baking. So it was only Auntie

Viv coming for tea. Poppy preferred it that way.

As soon as Edith's sister arrived, she wrapped Poppy up in a perfumey hug and planted sticky pink kisses all over her niece's face. "Wait till you see what I've bought you, Poppy. You're going to love it."

"Is it a new muffin tin like I asked for, Auntie Viv?"

"Don't be silly!" Auntie Viv chuckled, watching Poppy unwrap her present. "It's a briefcase for all your important spells and things. Now that you're going to be an Intermediate Witch, you've got to look the part. No more scruffy old backpack." While Poppy's parents oohed and aahed over the real leather briefcase, Poppy opened up the rest of her gifts. She got a new wand case, a miniature practice cauldron, and a DVD about famous witches. There was a picture of a scary-looking woman on the front cover, peering out from behind bars. It was called *Witches Who Strayed Off the Magical Path — A Close-up Look at Some Famous Witches Who Let Their Magic Lead Them Astray*.

"You'll enjoy that," Mrs. Pendle said. "It talks about what a big responsibility being magical is and how these witches abused their powers and became evil. Ended up on the dark side." She shuddered.

"So don't go getting any ideas!" her father joked. Poppy gave him a weak smile.

"Can we have my cake now?" she asked. "It's a new

recipe and I think you're all going to love it."

"Ooh, that's stunning!" Auntie Viv sighed as Poppy put a three-layer lemon cake on the table. It was covered in swirls of creamy frosting with yellow roses piped around the edge. Leaning toward her sister, Vivian whispered, "Poppy couldn't have made that. You must have got it from Patisserie Marie Claire."

"Of course Poppy made it." Edith Pendle frowned at Auntie Viv. "Although I told her it was bad luck, baking your own birthday cake."

"But I wanted to, Mum. It was fun."

"Yes, so let's all enjoy it," Edith said, thrusting forks around the table. "Because once Poppy's an Intermediate Witch, she'll be far too busy to bake. And no more reading cookbooks either." Edith Pendle sniffed. "Nothing but a waste of time."

Poppy didn't trust herself to speak. It was her birthday and she should have been happy, but she only felt sad as she sucked lemon frosting off her finger.

Chapter Three

....

Kibel Fallow Da

"STEP-UP TODAY!" MRS. PENDLE ANNOUNCED, FLINGING open Poppy's curtains. She straightened a framed print of her family tree that hung on Poppy's bedroom wall. "My parents were so disappointed when I didn't get the gift of magic," Edith Pendle said wistfully. "I tried and tried, but you either have it or you don't."

"I wish I didn't," Poppy whispered into her pillow.

After Mrs. Pendle had left the room, Poppy dragged herself out of bed and put on the clean uniform her mother had laid out. She trudged downstairs, stopping for a moment in front of the photo of Great-Granny Mabel that sat on the hall table, the one Poppy's parents said looked just like her. And although Poppy hated to admit it, even she could see the resemblance. They both had the same blue eyes and flyaway brown hair and an almost identical band of freckles sprinkled across their nose. Except the girl smiling back at her wore a purple graduation gown and clutched a rolled-up diploma. "I wish I'd known you." Poppy sighed. "Then perhaps I wouldn't be so mad at you!" After all, it wasn't Great-Granny Mabel's fault that Poppy had to go to Ruthersfield Academy, even though her great-grandmother had been the one to pass along the stupid witch gene. "Why couldn't you have been a baker?" Poppy whispered. "Then I would have wanted to be just like you."

Most mornings Poppy walked to school, but since today was the Step-Up Ceremony and it was pouring rain, Mr. and Mrs. Pendle insisted on driving her. As Poppy got into the car, she avoided looking at their custom-made license plate, which said WELUVRWTCH. Above it was a purple and gold bumper sticker declaring, PROUD PARENTS OF A RUTHERSFIELD GIRL.

"Well, you're really on your way now, love," Roger Pendle remarked. "Not a Novice anymore!"

Poppy watched as the local school bus rumbled past. A pale girl with a halo of frizzy curls had her face pressed against the glass. She looked about as lonely as Poppy felt. Perhaps if they both went to the elementary school, they could become friends. "I wish I were riding on that," Poppy whispered.

"No, you don't," Mrs. Pendle said firmly.

A sick, anxious feeling had lodged in Poppy's stomach, the way it always did when Ruthersfield came into view. The academy was an imposing stone building that looked more like a fortress than a school for witches. Flocks of older girls were landing their broomsticks gracefully on the pavement, and Poppy tripped as she got out of the car. Several of the girls tittered. "Don't forget your briefcase," Mrs. Pendle called after her. Grabbing it quickly, Poppy hurried off with her head down, trying to appear invisible. She could feel her socks start to slip, and using her free hand, Poppy gave them a quick tug, stumbling forward as she did so.

"Clunterpoke!" someone giggled behind her. Poppy could tell from the voice it was Deirdre Lambert, one of the popular girls in the seventh form. "Clunterpoke!" Deirdre taunted again, and Poppy bit down on her lip, trying not to cry. She was regularly called "clunterpoke," which in Ruthersfield slang meant "clumsy." It was, as Poppy had swiftly learned during her first year, an extremely unflattering term.

"Deirdre Lambert!" a sharp voice cut through the noise. "Apologize at once!" Turning around, Poppy saw Miss Corns, their magical management teacher, swoop down on a broomstick. "That sort of language will not be tolerated."

"Sorry," Deirdre mumbled, examining her purple fingernails. "It was only a joke."

"No, Deirdre, it was disrespectful. When you wear the Ruthersfield uniform, you represent the whole school. Your behavior mirrors what this academy stands for, and it does not stand for catty meanness."

Deirdre blushed. "I'm sorry," she muttered again.

"Very well." Miss Corns softened her voice. "Cobweb-sweeping duty after school for a week, please."

"A whole week? Every day?"

"Which means dusting well in all the corners."

"Yes, Miss Corns," Deirdre said, glaring at Poppy. This did seem rather a strong punishment, and Poppy gave her an apologetic smile. It was not well received. Deirdre narrowed her eyes and silently mouthed, "Cake head." Then, linking arms with another girl, she flipped back her long dark hair and flounced off. Not a good start to Step-Up Day, and as Poppy traipsed along behind them, she could feel the sharp metal clasp of the briefcase scraping against her leg.

✴ ✴ ✴ ✴

Inside the Great Hall, it sounded like a convention of spring robins. Only Poppy sat quietly, surrounded by twittering girls. As Ms. Roach walked onto the stage and stood with her arms folded, gradually the room fell silent. "Welcome, fourth formers," she began. "You have all been here for three years now, learning what it takes to become a witch, and today you are no longer Novices. Today you step up!" Excited whispering rippled through the crowd, and Ms. Roach waited until the room was silent again. "It is indeed an honor to become an Intermediate Witch, and the next few years will be challenging ones, requiring plenty of hard work and determination. We expect great things from our girls." Ms. Roach looked directly at Poppy, who had been dreaming about chocolate cream pie. Shifting in her chair, Poppy leaned forward, trying to focus, but it was difficult to stop her mind from wandering.

Smothering a yawn, Poppy shifted in her chair again as the headmistress's voice swelled. "But let us not forget that for hundreds of years witches have had a terrible reputation. They were considered evil and destructive, and were completely misunderstood, usually because of one or two genuinely wicked creatures. Now, of course, we have strict laws and regulations governing the art of magic and, as I'm sure you're well aware, our own maximum security prison especially for those witches who do not comply."

"Scrubs," Poppy heard Megan Roberts whisper. "If you end up in that prison, you never get out."

"Witchcraft has come a long way," Ms. Roach declared. "It is a highly respected profession these days, but as you prepare to step up to the next level, let me make one thing very clear." Here the headmistress paused a moment, staring at each girl in turn. "Black magic will not be tolerated," she said. "I repeat, black magic will not be tolerated. So, continue to practice your craft wisely, become the best witch you can be, and remember our school motto, girls."

"Kibet fallow da," the students chanted.

"Kibet fallow da," Ms. Roach warbled with emotion. "That ancient pagan saying written down by the first high priestess of magic. And we know what it means, don't we?" Ms. Roach held her arms wide as the girls yelled back.

"Follow your passion."

"Yes, and today, as you leave your Novice years behind, I ask all of you to do just that. To follow your passion and strive for excellence." Everyone applauded, although Poppy was deep in thought as she clapped her hands together, pondering whether dark chocolate or milk chocolate would make a better pie filling.

Chapter Four

Madeline Reynolds

I STAYED IN THE AIR FOR FIVE MINUTES," MEGAN ROBERTS bragged at the lunch table, "and my broomstick didn't even wobble." They had just come in from their first flying lesson, and Poppy was squashed at the end of the table, her long legs sticking out to the side. She was reading her newest *Good Eats* magazine, paying no attention to the conversation. Deirdre Lambert walked by and gave Poppy's shoe a light kick. As Poppy glanced up, Deirdre mouthed the words "clumsy clunterpoke," and gave a spectacular horsey sneer. The girls at the table giggled, and Megan Roberts whispered behind her hands, "Poppy is so weird!" Megan was flipping through the May issue of *Young Witch*, and had stopped at a page showing a smiling girl in a black-and-green-striped leotard, sitting astride a broomstick. At the top of the page, in bold letters, it said, TEN EXERCISES TO HELP YOU TONE YOUR BROOMSTICK-FLYING MUSCLES. Sucking in her stomach, Megan sat up straight and looked around the table. "Stomach in, shoulders back when you're riding a broomstick," she said. All the other girls copied, except for Poppy, who was staring at a glossy picture of a caramel tart.

"Poppy doesn't need to practice her exercises," Megan said, carefully balancing a spoon across the tip of her index finger. "She's been flying in secret."

"I have not!" Poppy said, feeling her face grow warm. "I've never even held a broom before today, except to sweep the floor with."

"Then how come you were so good?"

"I don't really know, but I didn't like it," Poppy admitted. "It actually made me feel a bit sick."

Megan smirked at her friend Fanny Freeman. "That's so dumb!" she said.

"I couldn't even get my broomstick off the ground," Fanny groaned, slumping forward over the table. "Being a Novice was so much easier. All this extra hard work they're piling on. I'm never going to graduate."

"Do you want to be a witch, then?" Poppy asked, and Fanny lifted her head to stare at Poppy.

"Of course I want to be a witch, cake head. What's the point of getting the gift if you don't use it?"

"I'm not sure," Poppy said softly, chewing the end of her braid. She didn't have an answer for that.

In history class, their first big project as Intermediate Witches was to pick one famous Ruthersfield alumna to write about. Poppy chose Madeline Reynolds, which caused quite an upset because she was a witch who had gone over to the dark side. Miss Jenkins, the history teacher, tried to steer Poppy toward someone else. "We have so many marvelous witches from our past to admire. What about Betty Tumly, who invented the lost-and-found tool? You simply program in what's been lost, a glove, your house keys, even your homework. Then sweep the finder around and it will beep when the missing item has been located. Or Katherine Jones?" Miss Jenkins suggested. "Now, there was an extraordinary woman. She used her magic to invent chocolate-flavored brussels sprouts, all the nutrition of regular sprouts but delicious for children to eat. And let's not forget your great-grandmother Mabel Ratcliff."

"Oh, I'll never forget her," Poppy said.

"That quick-growing hair potion she came up with is terrific for bald-headed men, and you can get it in such lovely colors." Miss Jenkins scrunched up her face in concern. "These woman were amazing, Poppy. Why pick Madeline Reynolds?"

"Because she interests me."

"She was head girl at Ruthersfield, a straight-A student, and then she went on to become the worst storm brewer in history. Joined the dark side. We had monsoon weather for six straight years until she was put behind bars." Miss Jenkins shuddered. "It was Madeline Reynolds who washed away the whole bottom half of Italy. Why would you write about someone like that?"

"To find out why she did it," Poppy said. "I think she must have been very unhappy." And then under her breath so Miss Jenkins couldn't hear, she whispered, "Maybe she didn't like being a witch."

That afternoon Poppy stayed late in the library, sitting at one of the long tables, surrounded by a stack of books on the life of Madeline Reynolds.

"You can check those out if you like," Miss Corns, the magical management teacher, said, poking her head around the door. It was strangely quiet. Even Ms. Gilbert, the librarian, had left.

"I know." Poppy looked embarrassed. "It's just easier to work here sometimes."

"Ahhhh." Miss Corns nodded. "Noisy brothers and sisters at home?"

"Not exactly," Poppy confessed. "I'm an only child, actually, but my parents like to watch me study, if that makes sense."

"They watch you study?" Miss Corns walked into the room. "I'm not sure what you mean."

Poppy gave a nervous laugh. "Well, they care a lot about me being at Ruthersfield, you see. My great-grandmother Mabel Ratcliff went here, and they want me to do well."

"And I'm sure you will," said Miss Corns.

"But they care so much about me being a witch that it's almost a bit, you know, smothering," Poppy finished guiltily.

"Smothering?" Miss Corns questioned, raising a gray, rather hairy eyebrow.

"My mum always sits in the same room with me when I'm doing my homework," Poppy explained. "She wants to keep me company, and she's very quiet because she doesn't want to disturb me, so she won't read because of the pages' rustling, and she doesn't knit or anything. So she just sits there and watches me." Poppy paused for a moment, then finished up. "It's a bit hard to concentrate when someone's staring right at you."

"I see," Miss Corns said, and judging from the sympathetic look on her face, Poppy got the feeling that she really did understand.

There was a companionable silence as Miss Corns moved around the room, straightening the odd book into place and dimming some of the lights. She paused in front of the long back wall, where a display of gilt-framed certificates hung. "Well, your great-grandmother Mabel certainly was an astonishing student," she commented. "Come and take a look, Poppy. She was voted Witch of the Year six times at school." Poppy got up and walked over to Miss Corns, who gestured at a row of certificates. Each one had Mabel Ratcliff's name engraved on it in perfect gold script.

"What do you have to do to be voted Witch of the Year?" she couldn't help asking.

"Simple," Miss Corns replied. "You have to be the best. Nothing short of perfect. And it's not just about the magic, either," she said, tapping at her chest. "It's about what's in here. You must be committed to your art, passionate about it."

"Well, I'll never be Witch of the Year." Poppy sighed. "Which will disappoint my parents no end."

"Oh, Poppy, you're an extremely talented young witch."

"Thank you." Poppy nodded glumly. Tucking a clump of loose brown hair back into one of her braids, she walked along the wall, staring at the names of past witches who had achieved this highest of honors bestowed on a Ruthersfield girl. Poppy stopped in front of an empty space where a dusty rectangular outline was still visible. "Why was this certificate taken down?" she asked Miss Corns.

"That was awarded to Madeline Reynolds." Miss Corns lowered her voice. "She went over to the dark side and became one of the most evil witches this century has ever seen. Ended up in Scrubs Prison. Hard to believe she got voted Witch of the Year. Although," Miss Corns admitted, "she was apparently rather famous for her spell chanting. Everyone always said Madeline Reynolds had the most extraordinary voice."

"Yes, she loved opera," Poppy added. "I'm studying her for my biography project."

"Indeed. That's an interesting choice." Miss Corns gave Poppy a strange look, but she didn't say anything further on the subject. "Turn the lights off when you leave, please, Poppy. The door will lock behind you automatically."

After Miss Corns had gone, Poppy sat back down at her table and stared at one of the books she had found. On the cover was a picture of the young Madeline

Reynolds, smartly dressed in her Ruthersfield uniform. She was smiling at the camera, but it was an automatic "say cheese" sort of smile that didn't reach beyond her mouth. Poppy was sure she could see a wistful longing in Madeline Reynolds's eyes, a sadness that made her wonder just how happy Madeline had been here at Ruthersfield. Maybe she hadn't wanted to be a witch either? Maybe her parents had forced her to study magic when what she really wanted to do was study opera? Sighing heavily, Poppy sketched a cupcake on the corner of her notebook, wondering what had gone wrong in Madeline Reynolds's life to send her over to the dark side.

....

Chapter Five

The Rescue of the Pink Sneakers

MRS. PENDLE WAS DELIGHTED WHEN POPPY GOT AN A ON HER biography project. "An original, in-depth essay," Miss Jenkins, the history teacher, had written in her comments. "Unusual but intriguing—congratulations!"

"Well done, sweetheart!" Edith Pendle said, smoothing out the crumpled pages Poppy handed her. She was sitting at the kitchen table with a cup of lukewarm tea. "Can't wait to show this to Daddy, although I still don't understand why you didn't choose Granny Mabel for your report." Mrs. Pendle glanced up at Poppy. "I mean, she's family after all, and that Madeline Reynolds was evil."

"I think she was sad more than evil," Poppy tried to explain. "Apparently, she loved opera." Then, in a softer voice, Poppy added, "But her parents thought singing was a waste of time." Mrs. Pendle made a huffing sound and scraped at a blob of dried-up cake batter that was smeared across the first page of Poppy's paper.

"You're lucky Miss Jenkins didn't take a mark off this for presentation," she said. "It may be well written, but it's a complete mess."

There was one thing Poppy did enjoy about Ruthersfield, and that was basketball. Ever since babyhood she had been gifted with the strange ability to jump unnaturally high, and from her first term at school, Poppy played on the basketball team. She was an excellent scorer, getting quite a reputation for her slam dunks, but because Poppy was as klutzy on the court as off, her legs were constantly covered in bruises. Even when her shoelaces were double knotted, she somehow managed to trip over her own feet. Still, Poppy loved the game, and it stopped her from thinking about magic. During recess she would practice shooting hoops, which meant she didn't have to hang about with Megan, Fanny, and the other girls, getting teased.

After most basketball practices, Poppy brought along something she had made as a snack. Her jam tarts and coconut cupcakes were popular, but it was the chocolate melt-away cookies that the team loved best.

"You must use magic in these!" Sandra Willis said, every time she ate one. "I've never tasted anything so good."

"No magic," Poppy would always say with a smile. "Just real vanilla essence and French cocoa."

One Thursday afternoon Poppy was walking home from school after practice. She stopped in front of Patisserie Marie Claire, as usual. There was something comfortingly familiar about the place, and Poppy had always felt drawn to the little French bakery, although she had never actually gone inside. She wanted to more than anything, but looking through the window was as far as Poppy got. She knew her parents would disapprove. They always bought their bread from Super Savers Market, sliced white loaves that had no taste. But it was more than that. Poppy also knew that if she opened the door and stepped into the patisserie, it would show her a world she could never be a part of, and that was too painful to think about.

A tempting selection of cakes and breads was displayed in the window, and Poppy pressed her face against the glass. She liked to watch the woman behind the counter, carefully wrapping up pastries in fancy white boxes. It would be wonderful to work in a shop like that, and Poppy sighed as the lights in the window went out. She had a physical ache in her chest, wanting so badly to learn how to make the cream-filled éclairs and little sponge cakes shaped like seashells. The woman who worked there smiled at Poppy as she hung a closed sign on the door. Poppy smiled back and slowly walked away. When she was a grown-up, maybe she would be brave enough to buy her bread at Patisserie Marie Claire—thick, knobby loaves of walnut wheat and long, crusty French baguettes.

As Poppy turned the corner onto Canal Street, she heard someone crying. A girl, probably about her own age, was sitting on the pavement, sobbing. She wasn't wearing any shoes. "What's wrong?" Poppy asked, squatting down beside her.

"They took my sneakers and threw them up there," the girl said, pointing to a tree. Poppy looked up and saw a pair of pink sneakers tied together at the laces and dangling over a high branch.

"Who did such a mean thing?"

"Some horrible girls in my class."

"You go to the elementary school, don't you?" Poppy said, recognizing the pale-faced girl with the frizzy hair. "I think I've seen you on the bus."

"Yes." The girl sniffed, wiping her sleeve across her

nose and staring at Poppy's purple uniform. "You go to Ruthersfield Academy."

"I do." Poppy looked uncomfortable. "I wish I didn't."

"Can you magic my sneakers down for me?"

"Don't need to," Poppy said, doing a few warm-up stretches. Then crouching low to the ground, she suddenly gave a powerful leap and jumped as high as she could.

"Wow!" the girl exclaimed as Poppy rocketed through the air and knocked the sneakers out of the tree. They plummeted straight down and almost hit the girl on the head. "Awwwh!" She blinked in shock. "That was amazing!"

"Gosh, I'm so sorry! Are you hurt?"

"No, I'm fine," the girl laughed. "How do you do that?"

"What, almost hit people?"

"No, I mean jump that high?"

"It's something to do with being magic." Poppy grinned. "I've always been able to jump like that and I'm strong, too, although you'd never know it, would you, with my skinny arms and legs! I'm Poppy, by the way."

"I'm Charlie," the girl said, smiling an enormous gappy smile. She had a rather large space between her two front teeth and pale, almost invisible eyebrows. "It's short for Charlotte. Charlotte Monroe."

"Would you like a cookie?" Poppy offered, taking a crumpled paper bag out of her briefcase. There was one chocolate melt-away left, which she had been saving for the walk home.

"Thanks." Charlie took a bite and groaned with pleasure. "That is scrummy! You must have bought these at Patisserie Marie Claire."

"I made them," Poppy said proudly.

"You did? How old are you?" Charlie asked, squinting shyly at Poppy. "I mean, you cook like a grown-up, but you're wearing a school uniform."

"I'm ten, but I'm tall for my age." Poppy shook crumbs from the bag into her mouth, managing to scatter most of them down the front of her sweater.

"Well, I'm ten too," Charlie said, "and look at me. I'm so short people think I'm still in the first form." The girls studied each other for a moment and then they both burst out laughing. "I'm also a terrible cook," Charlie admitted. "Maybe you could teach me? I know my mum would love that. She always eats my cookies because she doesn't want to hurt my feelings, but they taste disgusting. Yours are so good."

"My mum thinks cooking is a waste of time," Poppy said, scrunching the paper bag into a ball. "Witches aren't supposed to cook, but I don't want to be a witch. I want to be a baker."

"Ouch!" Charlie winced, trying to stand up. "I think I twisted my ankle when those girls pushed me over." She hopped about on one leg. "I can't put any weight on it."

"Careful." Poppy wrapped an arm around Charlie's waist. "Lean on me. I'll take you home."

"Are we going to fly on your broomstick?" Charlie sounded excited. "I've never flown on a broomstick before."

"Well, you're not missing much," Poppy said, lifting Charlie up onto her shoulders. Then grasping her briefcase in one hand and her broomstick in the other, Poppy set off with a skip. She immediately tripped and lurched forward, almost losing her balance.

"Are you sure we can't fly?" Charlie asked rather nervously, clinging to Poppy's braids. "I must be a bit heavy for you."

"No, no, you're fine," Poppy reassured her as they headed off down Canal Street. "Believe me, walking is much more pleasant."

By the time Poppy got home, it was beginning to get dark. She had walked right across to the other side of town carrying Charlie on her shoulders. They'd chatted and told jokes, and Charlie had listened to all Poppy's new recipe ideas. Talking to Charlie, Poppy felt as if she could truly be herself, and she was still feeling happy as she skipped up the garden path.

Edith Pendle opened the front door before Poppy had even reached for the brass knocker. "Where in heaven have you been?"

"I, um, basketball practice ran late," Poppy said, her happiness turning to guilt. She knew her mother would disapprove of Charlie because Charlie didn't go to Ruthersfield. "I'm sorry, Mum. I didn't mean to worry you."

"Oh, Poppy, you walked home, didn't you?" Mrs. Pendle sounded disappointed. "That's why you took so long."

Poppy sighed and shoved her broomstick in the umbrella stand. "I don't really like flying, Mum."

"But you're marvelous at it."

"I don't like flying," Poppy repeated. "It makes me feel sick, and I can't think when I fly. I'm too busy concentrating on not falling off. I'd much rather walk. It's relaxing and you see more."

"That's the silliest thing I've ever heard of, honestly." Mrs. Pendle frowned at her daughter. "Well, go and do your homework, Poppy. It's so late. You don't want to get behind."

"We don't have any tonight."

"You must have homework. It's a school night. How can you not have any homework?"

"We weren't given any, but I did get an A for my essay on the history of the wand," Poppy said, knowing this would please her mother.

"Oh, that's wonderful, Poppy!" Mrs. Pendle's frown disappeared, and Poppy made a dash for the kitchen. "Are you going to practice some of your spells?" Edith Pendle called after her. Poppy pretended not to hear. There was a recipe for almond crunch bars she wanted to try, and of course her mother wouldn't approve. Charlie, on the other hand, thought they had sounded delicious when Poppy described them to her on the walk home. You mixed marzipan into the batter. Poppy had promised to save her new friend some. They'd agreed to meet down by the canal tomorrow, so long as Charlie's ankle was feeling better.

"Just a strain," Charlie said after school the next day, holding up her bandaged foot for inspection. They were sitting on the low stone wall of an abandoned cottage that had been built alongside the canal. It had been empty for years. Part of the roof had fallen in and all the windows were broken. The canal was a man-made river cutting right through the middle of

Potts Bottom. Nowadays it didn't get much traffic. An occasional pleasure barge would steam by once in a while, but usually there were more ducks floating down it than boats.

"It's not too sore and I'm using my grandpa's walking stick," Charlie said. She was munching on one of Poppy's almond crunch bars. "Mmmm, these taste better than anything Patisserie Marie Claire sells."

"That's my dream," Poppy said, throwing a stone into the water. "To own a fancy cake shop when I grow up."

"Well, I'm sure you will. I'd buy things from you all the time."

"It's not as simple as that," Poppy explained. "My parents would never allow it. They're so proud of me being a witch, and I'm a good witch, a really good witch. That's the problem. It would break their hearts if I became a baker."

"Have you told them how you feel?" Charlie asked. "Sometimes parents can surprise you."

"You don't know my mum and dad," Poppy said miserably. "My mum hates it when I bake. She's even banned me from looking at my cookbooks. The only books I'm allowed to read are things like *Magic Through the Ages* and *The Art of Flying*."

"Oh, those do sound fun, though," Charlie said. "We

don't have anything like that in our house."

"You have to be a member of the Witches' Guild to join the Magic Book Club," Poppy told her. "They send me a new book every month. My parents signed me up when I was still a baby, if you can believe that. Apparently, I was the youngest ever person to join."

"Really!" Charlie looked impressed.

"I inherited the gift from my great-grandmother Mabel," Poppy explained. "Magic just happened to me when I was little. It wasn't something I could control."

"It must be sort of special though, being magic," Charlie said. "Flying about on a broomstick, casting spells. I wish I were. My life's so dull."

"I'll bet it's not. You just think it is. Believe me, magic doesn't make you any happier."

"Would you show me a spell?" Charlie begged. "I've never seen real magic before. Please?"

"Oh, fine," Poppy said, pulling her wand out of her briefcase. "But there's no substance to magic, you know. It's all hot air and showing off." Waving her wand over the canal, Poppy trotted out a quick spell. Suddenly hundreds of fish popped their heads above the water and started to dance. They jitterbugged and twisted and made kissing sounds at one another with fat, pouty lips. Charlie squealed with laughter as the fish boogied about, slapping and splashing with their tails. Then, waving their scaly fins at the girls, they flipped back underwater.

"That was unbelievable!" Charlie shrieked.

"Thanks"—Poppy gave a wan smile—"but it gets boring after a while." She sighed. "Believe me, I know."

Chapter Six

....

Just Say No

POPPY WAS LATE LEAVING FOR SCHOOL MONDAY morning, which had Mrs. Pendle flapping around the kitchen like a flustered hen.

"Miss Corns sent that letter home about today's magical management class being a special one, and could everyone please be on time. And here you are, Poppy, late again." Poppy had been up early baking lemon squares. She had hidden her *Good Eats* magazine with the recipe in it under her spell book so her mother wouldn't see. Mrs. Pendle had canceled Poppy's subscription to the magazine, so Poppy had to buy it from the corner shop now. The lemon squares had taken much longer than Poppy anticipated, and it was past nine o'clock by the time they were done. When Mrs. Pendle noticed the time, she snapped, "This is ridiculous," finally shooing her daughter out the door.

"Mum, I'm sorry," Poppy said, a warm container of lemon squares clutched against her chest. She could already feel her socks starting to slip as she hurried down the garden path. Maxine from next door was watching curiously from over the fence, a pink chiffon scarf tied around her curlers. It had started to drizzle lightly and Poppy wished she had grabbed an umbrella.

"Don't forget your wand!" Edith Pendle dashed after Poppy and tucked a sticky magic wand into her daughter's pocket. "No time to walk now, is there. You'll have to fly." Not wanting to upset her mother further, Poppy hopped onto her broomstick, balanced the lemon squares in her lap, and flew the short, rainy distance to Ruthersfield.

She made a rather slippery landing outside the school gates, skidding to a halt next to a small, dark purple van with no windows. It had DANGER—FEROCIOUS CARGO printed across both sides, and the license plate said SCRUBS 1. Poppy wondered why it was there, and feeling a touch nervous in case it had anything to do with her being so late, she hurried up the steps. She was actually relieved to see Deirdre Lambert rushing through the door just ahead of her. It was a nice feeling not to have to walk in alone. "What do you think is going on?" Poppy panted. "Did you see that van with the Scrubs license plates? I wonder why it's here. Do you think it's really from Scrubs Prison?"

"Don't you know anything?" Deirdre sneered. "Fourth years always get the Scrubs talk in May."

"What's that?"

"You're so dumb," Deirdre said, rolling her eyes at Poppy. "It's like, you know, the 'big speech' we all get," she whispered, lowering her voice and making quotation marks in the air with her fingers. "Some of the guards from Scrubs come all the way over here, just to talk to us. Tell us what it's really like in there." Deirdre picked at a corner of peeling purple nail polish. "It's meant to scare the pants off us so that we'll stay good, not abuse our powers."

"Oh, my goodness," Poppy murmured, shifting the lemon squares under one arm and nervously pulling up her socks. "That must be what Miss Corns arranged for this morning."

"Well, you'd better hurry then."

"Did it work?" Poppy couldn't help asking as she watched the older girl saunter off down the corridor. "I mean, scare the pants off you?"

Deirdre stopped and turned around. "Yeah, it

worked all right. It was horrible, really horrible. We're not allowed to talk about it, but I'll tell you this," Deirdre said. "It gave me nightmares for months afterward."

Poppy was undeniably nervous about entering her magical management class. She tapped lightly on the door and crept inside.

"You're late," Miss Corns said, glancing at the clock.

"I'm sorry, Miss Corns."

"Well, sit down quickly, please. I was just saying that we have some special guests visiting to talk with you all today. What you are about to hear is not to be discussed with any of the other students. Do you understand?"

"Yes, Miss Corns," the girls chanted.

"If any of you ignore this order, there will be swift and severe penalties. Am I clear?"

Before the girls could answer again, a loud knocking sounded on the door. It was immediately flung open, and a man dressed in a black guard's uniform marched in, followed by two other similarly clad men carrying an empty iron cage. There were no smiles or cheerful greetings as the cage was slammed onto the floor. The first guard shook Miss Corns firmly by the hand, and then he turned and addressed the girls. "Any of you know what this is?" he said.

"It's a cage," Megan Roberts answered.

"That is correct. Does anyone know what it's for?"

"Keeping wild animals in?" Fanny Freeman whispered.

"Close," the guard replied. He picked up a piece of chalk and wrote the word EVIL on the blackboard. "That cage is what you'll get carted off to Scrubs in if you misbehave. And some of our witches, like this one here," he continued, thrusting out a large, glossy photograph of a bald-headed woman, "never ever leave their cages." The witch's eyes were so wild and angry that Poppy actually pushed back her chair, scraping the legs across the floor.

"Calm down. It's only a photograph," the guard reminded them, propping the picture up on the blackboard next to the word EVIL. "She can't hurt you."

"Oh, but it's awful," Fanny Freeman wailed softly. She traced a sickle moon in the air with her finger. This was a sign the girls made whenever they saw or heard something distressing.

"Take a really good look at a very, very wicked witch," the guard said. "If you're ever tempted to dabble in black magic or misuse your powers, then I can promise you right now, that is how you're going to end up. Locked away forever."

"No!" Megan Roberts whimpered, but the guard slowly nodded his head.

"What you see there is a witch who went over to the dark side," he told them. Poppy stared at the photograph. The witch was wearing a purple boilersuit with a large black number ten printed on the front. "She wasn't always like this," the guard said. "At one time she was just like you lot, a good Ruthersfield girl. Head girl, if I'm right?" And he looked at Miss Corns for confirmation.

"Yes, indeed," she acknowledged in a quiet voice. "And believe it or not, one of our finest students."

"What did she do?" Megan whispered.

"Speak up," the guard barked. "I can't hear you."

Megan cleared her throat and tried again. "What did she do to end up in Scrubs?"

"She brewed storms. Powerful storms." The guard thumped the picture with his fist. "Whole bottom half of Italy is underwater because of her."

"Not Madeline Reynolds," Poppy gasped, trying to connect the wistful, smiling girl she had seen pictures of in books with this scary-looking creature.

"That's right," the guard said, striding right over to Poppy's desk. He smelled of tinned stew. "An A plus for the correct answer. You're a bright girl."

"I did a biography project on Madeline Reynolds," Poppy mumbled, looking away from the blackboard. Even though it was just a photograph, the witch appeared to be staring straight at her, and Poppy felt her face flush with heat. "Madeline Reynolds had a beautiful voice," Poppy said. "She loved opera, but her parents didn't want her to have a singing career."

"So what?" The guard shrugged. "That's not important. We're here to talk about the fact that she's evil, which is why she ended up in Scrubs Prison. No exercise allowed for this one. No freedom at all. Fed right through those bars like the wild creature she is." Pulling a bottle of water out of his pocket, the guard unscrewed the lid, tilted back his head, and proceeded to gulp down every last drop. He burped, wiped a hand across his mouth, and carried on speaking. "All prisoners at Scrubs get two meals a day, and it's always the same thing: water, porridge, and grapefruit."

"Why grapefruit?" one of the girls asked timidly.

"So they don't get scurvy. Nothing worse than a witch covered in scurvy. Their skin cracks and they get these awful bumps." The guard shivered. "Can't stand the sight of them, so we make sure they eat their grapefruit."

"How terrible," Poppy whispered. Then unable to stop herself, she asked, "Doesn't Madeline Reynolds ever get let out of her cage? Not even for a few minutes?"

"Nope, not that one, but she's a ten, one of our worst offenders," the guard said, gesturing at the photograph. "You see, we have a numbering system for all of our prisoners. If you're in for a more minor infraction like forecasting the stock market or fixing a football game, well, that makes you anything from a one to a five, depending on the severity of your crime. Those witches have more freedom. We let them out of their cages twice a day for job duty."

Fanny Freeman raised her hand. "What kind of jobs?" she asked.

"Sorting out the moldy grapefruit from the good grapefruit, peeling the grapefruit, and grinding up the rinds for compost with their fingernails."

"Oooh." Fanny made a face. "That's disgusting."

"Well, they're the lucky ones," the guard sneered. "If you're a six or higher, then you don't get to leave your cage, ever."

"What number would you get for turning someone into a toad?" a voice from the back of the class piped up.

"Depends." The guard cleared his throat. "We've got a witch in Scrubs at the moment who turned a whole family into hamsters. She's a seven, but it's the court's job to decide what number to give them. Our job is to make sure they don't escape. And in case any of you were wondering," he added, "all of our cages are housed in long, narrow buildings with no windows. Each cage is locked inside a soundproof cell so there's no communication at all between the prisoners. Meals are eaten in solitude, and there's no talking on job duty. The guards make sure of that."

"Can they have visitors?" Megan said.

"Absolutely not, and no letters from home, either. We don't allow our prisoners any contact with the out-side world." The guard started to walk slowly up and down the aisles. "Our exact location is top secret, as I'm sure you all know. The only information we give out is that we're on an island somewhere in the middle of the Pacific Ocean and"—here he pulled back his shoulders, beginning to swagger a bit—"I'm proud to tell you that our little island is fully self-sufficient. We grow all our own grapefruit and harvest an enormous oat crop twice a year for porridge."

"Truly impressive," Miss Corns murmured. The guard gave her a brisk smile.

"Just so as you're all aware," he suddenly barked, banging Fanny Freeman's desk and scaring some of the girls right out of their seats. "Once you're in Scrubs, you're in Scrubs for life. Got that?" he shouted, spitting out a spray of saliva with his words.

There was a long, drawn-out silence in the room until finally Miss Corns said, "Well, thank you for coming, Sergeant Murphy. I think the girls have heard enough." She looked as pale as the rest of her class.

"Happy to oblige," the guard replied, clicking his heels together. He strode toward the door and held it open while the two other guards picked up the cage and marched out. "And remember, girls," Sergeant Murphy said. "Just say no to evil. You do not want to end up in one of those."

As soon as the Scrubs party had left, Megan Roberts started to cry, loudly, and so did a handful of other girls. Poppy stared into space, feeling too stunned to make a sound. She couldn't believe what she had just seen, that horrifying picture of Madeline Reynolds. She also couldn't help feeling the tiniest bit sorry for the poor witch. Nobody should be subjected to a life like that, and although there had been hatred in Madeline Reynolds's eyes, Poppy felt certain she had glimpsed sadness in the photograph as well.

"Magic is a gift you have all been given, girls," Miss Corns said softly. "It's up to each one of you to manage it wisely."

"But what if we don't want to use our magic when we grow up?" Poppy questioned. "What if we want to do something else with our lives?" Miss Corns was silent for a minute, and then she gave a nervous laugh.

"My goodness me, Poppy Pendle. You do say the strangest things. For a moment there I thought you were serious." Poppy sighed and chewed at the end of her pencil. Even though she wasn't trapped in a real cage with iron bars, that's a bit how she felt right now, sitting inside Ruthersfield Academy, feeling so hot and stuffy she could scarcely breathe.

When Poppy met Charlie down by the canal later on that afternoon, she was in a gloomy mood. "It was an awful day," Poppy said, flinging her briefcase and broomstick at a patch of ferns and climbing on top of the wall. Poppy yanked the lid off the container of lemon bars and offered them to her friend. "I don't want to talk about it, because it was so horrible." Poppy picked up a handful of stones and threw them into the canal. She watched the circles ripple out, while Charlie sat beside her eating lemon bars. A goose waddled by, pecking at some crumbs on the ground. He gave a low honk, and Charlie giggled, throwing him a tiny corner of buttery crust.

"These are delicious," Charlie said softly, touching Poppy on the arm. A lump formed in Poppy's throat.

"I wish my parents thought so," Poppy said. "All they care about is magic." She scooped up another handful of stones and chucked them at the far bank. "I'm not even allowed to practice my cake decorating anymore, although using a piping bag requires just as much skill as a wand, if you ask me." Poppy sighed and added, "There's an interesting technique for buttercream frosting I'd like to try."

"Come to my house," Charlie suggested. "You can make it there if you like, and I'd love my mum and dad to meet you."

"Gosh, Charlie, can I?" Poppy spun round to face her friend, almost dropping the lemon bars. "That would be so great. Are you sure?"

"Of course I'm sure. It would be fun."

"Oh, Charlie, thank you, thank you so much, but don't tell them I'm magic," Poppy begged. "It always causes problems."

Chapter Seven

....

Time to Go

IT WAS NOT THAT DIFFICULT FOR POPPY TO PERSUADE her mother to let her go to tea at Charlie's house. For one thing, Poppy didn't mention the fact that Charlie was not a Ruthersfield girl. "I'm so glad you're finally making friends," Edith Pendle said happily. "Is she on the basketball team?"

"Ah, no, she's not exactly sporty."

"Is she in any of your classes?"

"She's the same age as me," Poppy said truthfully.

"I wonder if she's the first witch in their family? Do you know?"

"Mum, please." Poppy gave her mother an imploring

look. "We don't talk about that kind of stuff."

"Well, you must invite Charlie back to our house next week," Mrs. Pendle insisted. "We can show her our family tree."

Poppy had no intention of bringing Charlie anywhere near her parents, especially not after meeting Charlie's mum and dad. They didn't hover over the girls or badger them with questions about homework, and no one minded when Poppy sprawled on the floor next to Charlie, flipping through Mrs. Monroe's cookbooks. Afterward Mrs. Monroe even let them practice making chocolate buttercream in the kitchen. Then the whole family, including Charlie's mum and dad, spooned frosting straight out of the pan. This was something Poppy couldn't imagine doing with her own parents. Whenever she took out a mixing bowl at home, her mother's lips got all pursed. At Charlie's, Poppy felt completely happy, just like a normal girl.

"Please do come again," Charlie's mum said as Poppy reluctantly got ready to leave. "It's been a real pleasure meeting you, and Charlie was right. You're a wonderful baker. Your parents must be very proud."

"Oh, they are," Poppy agreed glumly, putting on her blazer. "They think I'm amazing."

At that precise moment the doorbell rang, and Poppy could see her mother's eager face peering through the glass panel. "Mum, what are you doing here?" Poppy said nervously as soon as the door opened. "I told you I'd walk home."

"I wanted to meet your friend's parents," Mrs. Pendle said, smiling so hard she looked uncomfortable. "These silly girls," she fussed. "Imagine walking when you can ride a broomstick." Charlie's mum seemed puzzled, and Mrs. Pendle added, "Poppy's top in her class at flying, you know."

"Flying?" Mrs. Monroe looked even more confused, and then her face cleared. "Oh, Poppy must go to Ruthersfield!" she exclaimed. "I had no idea, how exciting."

"And doesn't your daughter attend the academy?" Mrs. Pendle said.

"Heavens, no. We don't have enough magic in this family to bend a teaspoon!"

"Really!" Edith Pendle's lips tightened as she ushered Poppy outside, and she didn't speak again until they were in the car, driving home.

"What have you got all over you?" Edith finally snapped, glancing at Poppy in the rearview mirror. "You're covered in something sticky."

"Chocolate," Poppy admitted, not mentioning that

it was from a batch of frosting she had been allowed to make.

"Honestly!" Mrs. Pendle gave a succession of heavy sighs. "I'll have to give that a good soaking tonight."

"Mum, she's a nice girl," Poppy blurted out, wanting her mother to understand. "She's my friend."

"Poppy, she goes to the elementary school," Mrs. Pendle shot back. "Lots of girls are going to want to be your friend, simply because you're a witch."

"But Charlie's not like that. She doesn't care that I'm a witch, and she's funny, Mum. I really like her."

Mrs. Pendle gave another dramatic sigh. "You should have told me she wasn't a Ruthersfield girl. I trusted you, Poppy."

"Mum, if you knew she went to the elementary school, you wouldn't have let me see her," Poppy said, starting to cry.

"Listen, sweetheart." Mrs. Pendle's voice softened. "Daddy and I know what's best for you, and right now you really need to be concentrating on your magic." She reached back a hand and patted Poppy on the leg. "So for your own good, Poppy, you're not to see that girl again."

"But she's nice," Poppy said, huddling by the car window. "I like her, Mum. She's the only friend I've got."

"Oh, don't be so dramatic, Poppy. There are plenty

of nice girls at Ruthersfield. Girls just like you who are special."

"I don't want to be special," Poppy wept, kicking the back of her mother's seat. And then she said the words that had been building up inside her for months. "I don't want to be a witch." It felt so good, Poppy said them again, louder this time. "I don't want to be a witch, Mum. I hate magic." She could see the back of her mother's neck stiffen. "Mum, I truly don't want to be a witch," Poppy shouted. "Please try to understand."

"Now, Poppy, you're just having a bad day," Mrs. Pendle said at last. She switched on the radio. "We all get those once in a while."

Poppy kicked her mother's seat again in frustration. "It wasn't a bad day. It was one of the best days ever. I loved being with Charlie." Her mother didn't reply, and Poppy banged her fist on the door panel, needing to be heard. "Listen to me, Mum. I don't want to be a witch," she said, but her mother had turned up the volume, drowning out Poppy's words. Poppy slumped back with a sigh, sinking down in her seat. She saw her mother glance at her in the rearview mirror and turned her head away, feeling invisible.

As soon as they got home, Poppy charged straight upstairs. "I know you don't understand this now,"

Mrs. Pendle panted, following right behind her, "but you will when you're older, I promise. Charlie would be a distraction for you, and this is an important year, Poppy. You can't lose your focus."

"She's nice," Poppy sobbed, flinging herself down on her bed. "And Charlie's parents don't mind if she reads cookbooks."

"Charlie's parents don't have a little witch in the making, do they?" Mrs. Pendle clucked. "Now, how about this weekend we all take that trip to the Museum of Magical Discoveries I promised you? They have a whole display on Great-Granny Mabel and her hair invention."

"Mum, please go away," Poppy whispered, crying into her pillow. "I'd like to be alone."

"Well, there's no need to be rude, Poppy. I was only trying to be nice."

"Mum, I really hate magic," Poppy pleaded, lifting up her head and looking at her mother out of red, watery eyes. "I hate it. I hate it. You just never listen to me."

"I'm going to put the kettle on." Edith Pendle sighed. "Really, I'm just exhausted by all of this." She smoothed Poppy's skirt down. "Think about my museum idea, sweetheart. We could all do with a day out."

Poppy turned her face to the wall and closed her

eyes. Living here was unbearable. Nothing she said made a difference. Her mother would never understand how she felt.

"She doesn't recognize the opportunity she's got." Maxine from next door sympathized over a cup of tea later that afternoon. "What an honor it is to go to Ruthersfield. You've done everything for Poppy, Edith."

"We have." Mrs. Pendle nodded, dabbing her eyes with a tissue. "And Ruthersfield's not cheap, let me tell you! I'm not complaining, mind you, but I do wonder sometimes if Poppy really appreciates what we're giving up for her."

"Yes, and I've never heard you complain once," Maxine remarked.

"Well, you want what's best for your child, don't you, and that Charlie —" Mrs. Pendle inhaled, gripping the edge of the table so tightly her knuckles turned white. "I'm sure she's the one who's been putting ideas into Poppy's head, turning her against her magic." She leaned forward. "I don't mean to sound hard-hearted, Maxine, but Poppy is not to see that girl again."

"Oh, I couldn't agree more. She'll thank you in the long run," Maxine murmured.

"And all this nonsense with cooking," Mrs. Pendle

said, watching Maxine help herself to one of Poppy's dream bars. "I can't take it anymore. It has to stop."

"Mmmmmmm," Maxine moaned, chewing slowly on the dream bar. It was one of Poppy's own creations. "These are sensational, though. You can't deny she cooks like an angel."

Picking up the plate of chocolate marshmallow fingers, Mrs. Pendle walked over to the sink and dumped the whole lot in. Then she turned the water on full blast and shoved the rest of the dream bars down the trash disposal.

When Mr. Pendle got home from work that evening, Mrs. Pendle met him at the door, sniffing tearfully. He took off his shoes and put on his slippers while his wife told him exactly what to say. "You must be firm with her, Roger. For her own good. I've tried to explain things to Poppy, but she needs to hear it from her father."

"Right."

"She has to understand we know what's best for her."

"Okay." Roger Pendle looked a little puzzled.

"Tell her we won't put up with any more of this nonsense. Make it clear she can have Ruthersfield girls over whenever she wants, but not that Charlie person from the elementary school, and no more baking."

"Well, now, that's a bit harsh, isn't it?" Mr. Pendle blew his nose.

"But it's so disruptive to her studies."

"Not even the odd cookie or something? After she's done her homework?"

"She's a witch, Roger. That's what she needs to be concentrating on now. Unfortunately, it's never just the odd cookie with Poppy."

"Yes, you're right," Mr. Pendle agreed. "We must be firm." And squaring his shoulders, he marched upstairs to talk to Poppy.

"Well, how did she take it?" Mrs. Pendle asked over dinner that evening. Poppy had refused to leave her room and join them.

"Oh, she understands," Mr. Pendle said, forking up shepherd's pie and trying hard not to taste what he was swallowing. It was Super Savers's own brand and had the smell and texture of canned dog food. "She's a bit upset, of course," he added, stirring his dinner around. "But not as angry as I was expecting. I have to say I'm rather proud of myself. Yes." He straightened his tie and smiled across at his wife. "I believe she took it very well, Edith."

Upstairs in her room, Poppy threw some clothes into a pillowcase along with her favorite cookbooks and basketball. A deep sadness swelled inside her. She couldn't stay here anymore, not after the awful conversations with her parents. Besides never seeing Charlie again, her father had told Poppy in the nicest possible way that she wasn't going to be allowed to do any more cooking, either. "And I love to bake," Poppy whispered. "I just love it." The thought of never making another cupcake again was too much for her. Wiping away the last of her tears, Poppy ripped out a blank page of her spell journal and scrawled across it in purple ink.

Dear Mum and Dad,

I have run away from Potts Bottom. Please don't try to find me, because I'm not coming home. Ever. I don't want to be a witch and I hate magic. I HATE IT. I'll never be like Great-Granny Mabel.

Love, Poppy

Leaving the note lying on her bed, Poppy softly opened her bedroom window and looked down. If only her parents could accept who she was and be happy for her. If only they didn't care so much about her magic. But they did, and there was nothing Poppy could do to change that. She hesitated a moment as she pondered the drop. It was too far to jump, but she had no intention of walking downstairs and out through the front door. Her parents would find a way to stop her. With a resigned sigh, Poppy picked up her magic wand and quickly conjured up a rope ladder. She didn't like using magic, but this was an emergency. Then, throwing the pillowcase over her shoulders, and without a backward glance, she scrambled to the ground.

Lights were shining through the kitchen window, and Poppy could see her parents staring at the television. The opening credits for *Magic in the Family* were just starting up, and a box of disgusting, artificially flavored, chocolate-filled chocolate cakes called Fudge Monkeys sat between them. Poppy blinked back tears, refusing to cry anymore. A torrent of hot anger suddenly swept through her, and the force of such powerful emotion scared Poppy. She was right to run away. This sort of anger wasn't good. Not wanting anything more to do with magic ever again, she hurled her wand with all her strength into some rhododendron bushes. It landed with a soft plop, and turning to give one final look at the house on Pudding Lane that had been her home for the past ten years, Poppy clambered over the garden fence and started to head toward town. Although she felt scared and alone, Poppy kept on walking. She had to be able to bake.

Chapter Eight

....

Patisserie Marie Claire

POPPY KNEW EXACTLY WHERE SHE WAS GOING. Patisserie Marie Claire had no lights on, but coming from the apartment above was the sound of opera music. Giving a gentle knock, Poppy held her breath and waited. There was no response. Feeling her heart start to race, she knocked more loudly. She kept on knocking until a door in the back of the shop opened and a woman appeared. It was the same woman Poppy always saw serving behind the counter. She was wearing an elegant pink silk dressing gown. As the lights flicked on, Poppy could see that she didn't look too happy at being disturbed. "We're closed," the woman said, unlocking the front door and folding her arms across her chest. She frowned and studied Poppy, a puzzled expression on her face.

"I know, and I'm really sorry to disturb you, but I was wondering if you needed any help."

"It's so late," the woman said in a faded French accent. "Help with what? Have we met before? You seem familiar to me."

"I-I don't think so," Poppy stammered, shifting about from foot to foot. Her socks had slipped down again, and she wished she had tucked in her shirt before knocking. "I just thought you might need some help with the baking?" Poppy knew how she must look with her pillowcase full of stuff. "I'm a good cook, I really am."

The woman stared hard at Poppy, taking in her tearstained face and messy hair. "Are you sure I haven't seen you somewhere before?"

"Well, I walk by here quite a lot," Poppy admitted.

"What is your name, child?"

"P-Poppy."

"Shouldn't you be at home doing your homework, Poppy?" the woman asked suspiciously. "You seem awfully young to be out looking for work." Poppy felt her face grow warm. This wasn't going the way she had hoped at all. Blinking back tears, Poppy stood up really straight. At least she was tall for her age. Maybe the woman would think she had graduated.

"I am older than I look. I go to, I mean, I used to go to Ruthersfield Academy. I've left now," Poppy said, sounding flustered. "Magic wasn't really my thing." The woman didn't look convinced, and Poppy took a deep breath, trying to steady her voice. "I want to learn how to be a proper baker," she added with passion. "Just like you."

"Just like me!" the woman mused, giving a small smile, but still not opening the door any wider.

"Here, try one of these," Poppy said, taking a rectangular-shaped cookie from her pocket. It had crumbled at the edges and was covered in bits of fluff. The woman sniffed it cautiously.

"Go on, please try it," Poppy begged. "Almond butter crunch. It's my own recipe."

The woman nibbled a corner and chewed. Then she took a proper bite and closed her eyes. People often did that when they tried Poppy's cooking. "This is delicious. It's buttery and crunchy. . . . *C'est magnifique*."

"Does that mean I can stay?" Poppy asked hopefully. "Just for the night?"

"Do your parents know you're here?" the woman said.

Poppy stared down at the ground, trying to decide

how to answer. She chewed on her thumbnail and finally whispered, "They didn't want me to make a career out of baking." She swallowed the lump that had risen in her throat, and in a trembly voice added, "I can't go home. I just can't. And I've nowhere else to go."

"Ahhhhhhhh." It was a long, drawn-out ahhhhhh. The woman nodded. "I believe I understand now. Well, you had better come in," she said kindly, stepping aside so Poppy could pass. "It's not good to be wandering the streets at this hour."

The woman, whose name was Marie Claire Gentille, took Poppy through to the kitchen, where all the pastries and breads were made. It was spotlessly clean and an enormous dishwasher hummed softly. Marie Claire frowned. "I'm afraid my little apartment is tiny, and I don't really have anywhere for you to sleep. But just for tonight I can make you a bed up in here."

Poppy hoped she wasn't going to start crying again. "I would so like to stay here and help you with the baking, please." She dropped her pillowcase on the floor and her basketball rolled out. Poppy clasped her hands together. "Please, please, please let me stay," she pleaded.

Marie Claire narrowed her eyes, watching Poppy closely. She didn't answer straightaway. The silence grew and grew, until finally, just as Poppy couldn't bear it any longer, Marie Claire said softly, "You will need to call your parents right now and tell them where you are."

"I'll do it, I promise," Poppy said in a rush. "But you don't understand what they're like," she whispered, chewing the end of her braid. "You have no idea."

Marie Claire's voice was serious. "Maybe I don't. But it is important you let them know you are safe, Poppy." She held Poppy's gaze steadily.

"Okay." Poppy nodded, understanding that she had no choice about this.

"Very well, then, *chérie*." Marie Claire offered Poppy a tissue. "Perhaps for a few days, until we sort this out, I could do with a little help in the kitchen."

"Oh, thank you, thank you," Poppy said, realizing she had been holding in her breath all this time. She shivered with happiness. "I can't believe I'm actually going to be working at Patisserie Marie Claire!"

"But first you must call your parents," Marie Claire said, handing Poppy a slim, scarlet phone. "And then I can speak with them myself."

"Oh, no!" Poppy shook her head, looking scared. "You can't do that. Please. Not yet."

Marie Claire rested a hand lightly on Poppy's shoulder, her eyes full of sympathy. "All right, Poppy," she said. "I will give you a little privacy while you talk. If you need me, I shall be in the shop."

Poppy had no idea what she was going to say. The phone rang and rang, and Poppy guessed that her parents were probably still watching *Magic in the Family*. She knew how much they hated being disturbed during their favorite shows. When she heard her mother's loud voice announcing, "You have reached the Pendle family, Roger and Edith and our brilliant little witch. Please leave a message after the beep," Poppy whispered into the mouthpiece, "It's me. I'm okay and I'm not coming home, so please don't worry." She sniffed and pressed the off button, relieved that she had kept her promise to Marie Claire. Her parents were bound to come looking for her, but she was safe at the patisserie for now.

"You won't be all that comfortable," Marie Claire remarked, looking around the kitchen with her hands on her hips. "Give me a moment, though." She disappeared upstairs and returned with a camp bed and blankets. "We can set this up over here," Marie Claire said, putting the bed down in a corner of the room. "That way you'll have your own little space."

"Oh, it's perfect!" Poppy told her. "I'll be so warm, and it smells delicious. Kitchens are my favorite places in the world. I can't believe I'm actually going to be sleeping in one!"

"Like little Cinderella!" Marie Claire smiled, shaking her head. "Except you'll be covered in flour and not ashes! And I must warn you," she added. "I get up at four every morning. That's when I bake all my breads and croissants."

"I don't mind," Poppy said. "Honestly, I'd love that. I really would. I'm dying to know how you make croissants. And once I've learned how to get the breads and things started, you could sleep in later," Poppy chattered. "I'd bring you tea in bed."

Marie Claire laughed softly. She spread the blankets over Poppy's bed. "Try to get some rest now, *chérie*. You must be tired. And tomorrow we will be up extra early because on Wednesdays I make a wonderful chocolate butter bread."

Poppy lay down on the camp bed. Even though it was narrow, she slept soundly and didn't wake up until the sound of Marie Claire's singing roused her. It was still dark outside, and Marie Claire handed her a steaming cup of milky coffee. Poppy sipped cautiously. She had never had coffee before, but this was delicious. It would make a wonderful flavoring for cupcakes, she decided.

"I slept really well, Marie Claire," Poppy said,

getting out of bed at once. Her braids were messy and she had gone to sleep in her clothes. But Poppy couldn't stop smiling.

"I am glad. You look rested." Marie Claire smoothed a hair back from Poppy's face. "And later on when it is not so early, we need to talk, *chérie*." Poppy gave a vague nod in reply. "I will help you work this out," Marie Claire reassured her. "Everything will be fine."

"I know it will be," Poppy answered softly. "Because I'm here now."

"Right, then, first we will work on our bread doughs," Marie Claire said, scooping flour into an enormous bowl. "They need the longest time to rise. Now, take this chocolate and chop it for me, please." Poppy did as she was told. Soon the kitchen was filled with the rich, yeasty smell of bread rising and baking. Marie Claire showed Poppy how to roll out croissant dough and shape it into crescents. Some were left plain. Others they filled with almond paste or stuffed with custard and raisins. Poppy learned to make a soft, buttery bread dough called brioche, into which they stirred chunks of bittersweet chocolate. "My famous chocolate butter bread," Marie Claire said, putting a tray of loaf pans into the oven. "People come from many towns all over to buy this. I only make it on Wednesdays."

"If people love it so much, why not make it every day?"

"Then it wouldn't be so special"—Marie Claire winked—"and on Wednesdays everyone needs a treat. It is a day when sad things often happen, I have found." Poppy laughed, although she wasn't sure if Marie Claire was joking or not.

After the chocolate butter bread had finished baking, Marie Claire cut them each a slice. "Now we taste to make sure it is good." She motioned for Poppy to sit down. "You should never eat standing up or walking around. It is not good for the digestive system. Plus, you never taste your food properly if you are moving about. We want to sit and concentrate." Marie Claire closed her eyes and took a bite. Poppy copied her. She could feel the warmth of the morning sun streaming through the windows.

"This is perfect," Poppy sighed, chewing slowly. The bread was soft and airy. You could really taste the creamy French butter Marie Claire insisted on using. Chunks of dark chocolate melted on Poppy's tongue. When she swallowed, she knew this was one of the most delicious things she had ever eaten.

"That's my dream," Poppy whispered with longing. "To cook like that and have a bakery of my very own."

"And I'm sure one day you will," Marie Claire replied, gently touching Poppy's arm. "But now it is time to set up the shop. We open in thirty minutes."

They filled the glass cases and window displays with trays of breads and pastries. Then Marie Claire handed Poppy a pink-and-white-striped apron. "Put this on, *chérie*. We wear these when we serve."

"Oh no, I couldn't!" Poppy froze behind the counter. She was staring through the window and her eyes were full of panic. People had already started to gather outside, and standing at the front of the line was nosy old Maxine from next door. "I don't want to be out here," Poppy said, and dropping her apron on the floor, she hurried back into the kitchen.

Chapter Nine

....

Caramel Cookies

LATER, WHEN MARIE CLAIRE APPEARED IN THE KITCHEN doorway, Poppy explained, "I'd much rather wash dishes, and my math is terrible. I don't want to handle the money."

"Really," Marie Claire mused, watching Poppy scrub away at a mixing bowl. Drops of brown water had sloshed onto the floor, and when Poppy put the bowl in the drying rack, streaks of chocolate still clung to it. "You'll get lonely, being in here all by yourself."

"No, I won't," Poppy said. "I love your kitchen, and

perhaps when I've washed up these pans, I could start baking cookies?" The shop bell tinkled.

"I must go," Marie Claire said, turning to leave. "Someone needs serving."

"So can I?" Poppy called after her. "Bake some cookies, that is?"

"Well, I can't promise we'll sell them, but all right, go ahead," Marie Claire agreed, glancing back to give Poppy a friendly smile. As she opened the shop door, she whispered under her breath, "What have I gone and done? This could be a complete disaster." But Marie Claire was still smiling as she wrapped up a loaf of chocolate butter bread and handed it over to her customer.

Poppy had been thinking about caramel cookies for a long time now. How they would taste and how she would make them. There were no recipes for caramel cookies in any of her cookbooks, so she made one up as she went along. Plenty of butter and brown sugar, a pinch of salt, and some fresh vanilla beans ground to a powder.

"Whatever you're making, it smells fantastic," Marie Claire said, untying her apron and collapsing into a chair. Each day she closed the patisserie for two hours at lunchtime.

"Try one," Poppy said shyly, offering Marie Claire a cookie.

"*Mon Dieu!* You made a lot," Marie Claire gasped, staring at the counters. "A lot of cookies and a lot of mess!"

"I'm sorry. I got a little carried away, but I'll clean it all up, I promise," Poppy assured her. She felt nervous as she watched Marie Claire chew. The French woman didn't say anything for what seemed like an awfully long time. Then she gave a brisk nod.

"Excellent, Poppy. Arrange some on a plate and we'll see how they sell."

"Really? You're going to put my cookies in your shop?" Poppy spun around in excitement, knocking a bag of flour onto the floor. "Oh my goodness. I'm so sorry. I'll sweep that right up," she said, reaching for a broom. "I'm just so happy! I can't believe it. I'm a real cook."

Marie Claire laughed. "Please let me sweep. It will be quicker."

"Are you sure? It is my mess."

"Quite sure," Marie Claire said, tugging the broom out of Poppy's hands. "Why don't you take that basket-ball of yours out back? I put up a hoop for my son when he was younger. He used to play all the time before he left for college. It will be nice having it used again." She smiled at Poppy. "Go on, some fresh air will do you good."

Cautiously opening the kitchen door, Poppy stepped outside. She found herself standing in a small courtyard with a basketball hoop attached to one wall. Flowers had been planted in big wooden barrels, and purple clematis climbed freely up the back wall of the bakery. A small round table and chairs were tucked into a corner, shaded by a green umbrella. It was a lovely, tranquil place, and Poppy played ball until Marie Claire joined her, carrying a tray of sandwiches and lemonade. They sat at the little table and ate slowly, chatting about recipes.

"Perhaps now would be a good time for me to call your parents?" Marie Claire said when Poppy had finished her lunch. "I do need to talk to them, Poppy."

"No." Poppy shook her head vigorously. "I mean, not yet." Her bottom lip started to tremble. "It's awful at home. You've no idea how horrible it is."

"Do they know how you feel about things?"

"I've tried to tell them, but they don't listen to me," Poppy said, staring at the table.

"You should write it down," Marie Claire suggested gently. "Sometimes it is easier for parents to hear what their child is saying in a letter. It might help them understand how you are feeling. And then I can speak with them about it." Marie Claire sounded so confident and sure that Poppy suddenly felt a small glimmer of hope. Maybe this kind, lovely French person could convince her parents that she wasn't meant to be a witch. That magic was not her destiny. But that brief wishful thought quickly vanished. Her mother and father would never agree to such a thing. Poppy knew that. She was quiet for a long moment, and then she slowly nodded. Besides, it wasn't Marie Claire's problem, it was hers.

"Okay," Poppy agreed. "I'll write to them." That couldn't hurt. But what she didn't tell Marie Claire was that she had no intention of letting her parents know where she was. They would march right down to the patisserie and drag her back home.

"You are doing the right thing, Poppy," Marie Claire said, leaning over to pat Poppy's hand. "And ask them to contact me, straightaway. Then we can sort all this out." She gave Poppy a reassuring smile. "There's a postbox outside the back gate."

Later on that afternoon Poppy sat down at the big wooden table in Marie Claire's kitchen, and after chewing the end of her pencil for a few minutes, she began to compose a letter to her parents, explaining why she had run away.

Dear Mum and Dad,

Please don't be mad at me. I am safe and very happy. The kind lady I am staying with would like to talk to you, but before she telephones I want to tell you why I ran away. I hope you will understand and not be cross.

Ever since my first day at Ruthersfield, I've been so miserable at school. I keep trying to tell you how much I hate magic but you don't seem to hear. So let me spell it out for you: I DO NOT WANT TO BE A WITCH. The other girls tease me because I'm not like them, and call me names because I love to bake all the time. That's why having Charlie as my friend is so important. I was really, really, lonely until I met her, and you can't take Charlie away from me. You just can't.

Every day I wake up and feel sad because I know how much you hate it when I cook. I can't even talk to you about recipes I invent, because it makes you angry. So this is how I feel, Mum. When I bake a new cookie or cupcake I get all tingly inside and want to dance and sing and jump up and down all at once. I wish you could understand and weren't always so disappointed in me. I know I am never going to be like Great-Granny Mabel, although sometimes I wish that I were. Then perhaps you might be proud of me.

Love, Poppy

There was nothing in the letter they didn't already know, but maybe, just maybe, Poppy thought wistfully, they would read it and understand. When she had finished, Poppy folded up the pages and slid the letter into an envelope. She printed "Mr. and Mrs. Pendle, 10 Pudding Lane, Potts Bottom" on the front. It was only as she was about to creep out to post it that Poppy realized her parents would see where it had been mailed from. Then they would know she was still in the village, and be bound to find her. Not sure what else to do, Poppy slipped the letter into her pocket. *For now,* she told herself.

The caramel cookies were a huge success. They sold out completely. "Everybody loved them," Marie Claire said as they tidied up the shop at the end of the day. "One woman told me they were the best-tasting cookies she'd ever eaten."

Poppy, who was pushing a mop enthusiastically across the floor, couldn't stop smiling. "I feel so at home, Marie Claire." She breathed in deeply. "Even the smell of this bakery is comforting. It makes me feel like a baby inside, all safe and warm."

"Maybe that's because you're standing right where a little girl was born," said Marie Claire.

"Right here?" Poppy looked down, as if there

might still be traces of a baby left on the floor. "A real baby?"

"As real as they get," Marie Claire said, remembering that strange and special day. "She ate a whole bag of my almond cakes. I've often wondered what happened to her." She sighed and shook her head. "The parents never did come back to tell me. Ah well, it is as it's destined to be, I suppose." Poppy didn't really understand what Marie Claire meant by this, but she could tell that the Frenchwoman was lost in her thoughts.

A peaceful silence settled on the shop until Poppy said softly, "It must have been wonderful for your son to grow up here."

"He liked it well enough, but Pierre is not a cook. Flying is his great love." Marie Claire gave a resigned smile. "He would help out when I needed it, of course, but there was no passion there. That's what a truly great baker must have," she said, holding both hands over her heart. "Passion!"

"Kibet fallow da," Poppy burst out. "That was our school motto. It means to follow your passion."

"And so you are, *chérie*. Love is what makes my bread so good, and you have that passion. You have great talent."

"Do I really?" Poppy said, hardly daring to believe what Marie Claire was telling her.

"Indeed you do, child." And if Poppy could have smiled any wider, her face would have split in two. "I will help your parents understand," Marie Claire continued. "Perhaps we can arrange it so that you can make your special caramel cookies every Wednesday after school. It will be something nice for the customers to look forward to."

"Oh, and I could make coconut cupcakes on Mondays." Poppy suggested, clapping her hands with enthusiasm. "Or coffee cupcakes, perhaps. I have a wonderful idea for coffee cupcakes. And how about chocolate melt-aways on Thursdays? Everyone always loves those. And raspberry jam shortbreads on Fridays?"

Marie Claire shook her head and laughed. "One recipe at a time, Poppy, one recipe at a time. It all sounds quite delicious though, *chérie*. I am sure you will make the customers very happy!"

The next day Poppy woke at four o'clock to help Marie Claire get started on the bread doughs. She loved being in the kitchen at such an early hour, the heavy quiet and the dark outside. At around five thirty she put a tray of cherry scones in the oven, and when the sun rose Poppy and Marie Claire sat by the window nibbling on the fresh, warm pastries. It was a perfect moment. And so the day began.

Poppy was careful not to appear in the front of the shop. She couldn't risk having nosy old Maxine from next door see her and report back to her parents. It was most important she stay hidden in the kitchen, out of sight.

Chapter Ten

....

Surprise

LATE ON THURSDAY AFTERNOON, MARIE CLAIRE APPEARED in the kitchen, a puzzled look on her face. "There is a person out front wanting to see you, Poppy."

"Are you sure?" Poppy said, sinking down on a chair. Her mouth felt as if it were full of cotton wool. "Maybe they meant someone else? It can't be me," she added shakily.

"She asked if someone called Poppy was here," Marie Claire stated, watching Poppy closely. Then holding out her hand, she said in a gentle voice, "Come, *chérie*. There is nothing to fear. I will take you." Getting unsteadily to her feet, Poppy clasped Marie Claire's warm, flour-dusted hand and followed her out of the kitchen.

It was such a relief to see Charlie's smiling face that Poppy didn't know whether to laugh or cry. She started to do both as Charlie skipped behind the counter and wrapped her friend up in an enormous hug. "I'll be upstairs if you need me," Marie Claire said softly. She gave Poppy a long, thoughtful look. "No reason why we shouldn't close a few minutes early today." And flipping over the OPEN sign, she left the girls in peace.

"Where have you been? I waited outside Ruthersfield yesterday and today and you weren't there. I thought you were sick until this funny man came by my house, asking all these weird questions about you. A private investigator," Charlie said, lowering her voice.

"How do you know he was a private investigator?" Poppy whispered, even though they were alone in the shop.

"He showed me his card. It had 'PI Jones' on it or something like that."

"So what did he ask?" Poppy worried, chewing the end of her braid.

"How long I'd known you. If I had any idea where you might have gone. That kind of thing." Charlie paused and glanced at Poppy. "Then he told me to call him right away if I heard anything from you. He said your parents had hired him to find you because they don't want anyone to know that you've run away and they don't want the police getting involved just yet."

"Of course they don't," Poppy said sadly. "That would be far too revealing, wouldn't it? Their own daughter running away because she doesn't want to be a witch. What would Ruthersfield Academy think about that?"

"You've really run away, then?"

"Yes, and I'm not going back, Charlie. You must promise not to tell." Poppy gripped her friend's hands. "Honestly, I'll die if I have to go home. I love it here. I'm so happy."

"Of course I won't say anything," Charlie promised. "I'm just so glad I've found you. It's been miserable, Poppy. Finally I make my first real friend and then she goes and disappears on me."

"How did you know where I was?" Poppy asked. "I haven't left the kitchen."

"Your chocolate cookies gave you away." Charlie grinned, holding up a white paper bag. "One bite and I knew who had made them. So I asked that nice lady if you were the cook."

"Well, I'm so pleased you did," Poppy said, realizing

how much she had missed her friend, even though it had been only two days.

A sudden flash of purple caught Poppy's eye, and she saw a girl in a Ruthersfield uniform walking by the shop. Poppy gasped and immediately dropped to the floor. "Come on, it's not safe here. Let's go out back." Crawling on her hands and knees, she pushed her way through the swinging door into the kitchen.

"You can't hide here forever," Charlie said, following behind her friend.

"Yes, I can," Poppy said, getting to her feet and brushing flour off her knees. "I'm never leaving Marie Claire's."

"Where do you sleep?" Charlie asked, and Poppy pointed to the camp bed in the corner. Soft flannel-covered pillows and sheets gave it a cozy feel, and her cookbooks were stacked on a little wooden shelf beside it.

"In the kitchen?"

"Oh, I love it, Charlie! It's warm and it smells so good." Poppy took some butter that was softening on the counter and emptied it into a mixing bowl. "The best part is, I get to cook all day long."

"No more magic?" Charlie said a little wistfully.

"Nope!" Poppy shook her head. "Never again. I threw my wand away."

"You did?"

"Don't look so shocked, Charlie. You know I hated doing magic." Poppy started to giggle as she spooned powdered sugar into the bowl. "Raspberry jam shortbreads, I think." As she stirred the butter and sugar together, a swirling rainbow cloud formed and rose out of the bowl. It hovered above the table for an instant before popping and sending down showers of multicolored candy sprinkles.

Charlie laughed. "I thought you said no more magic! How do you do that?" she asked, pressing a finger into the sprinkles and tasting them. "Mmmm, sweet."

"I can't help it." Poppy shrugged. "It doesn't happen much. Usually when I'm feeling really happy about something." She smiled at her friend. "It's probably because you're here."

"Except I've got to go in a minute, because we're having supper with my gran," Charlie said. "She lives over in Ribbleswold. But can I come back and see you tomorrow, after school?"

"Come whenever you like. Marie Claire won't mind, and I'd love it." Poppy was silent for a moment. "Charlie, could you do me a favor?" she said, pulling a creased envelope out of her pocket. She offered it to her friend, who took the sticky paper gingerly in her fingers, trying to avoid the streaks of frosting.

"What is this?"

"It's a letter," Poppy explained. "To my parents. I told Marie Claire I would write to them. The only problem is, I can't post it, can I, because if I do, they'll see it's been mailed from Potts Bottom. Then it won't take them long to find me, not with a private investigator looking. So I'm thinking you might post this from Ribbleswold if you're going? It's a much bigger town than Potts Bottom." Poppy hesitated a moment. "You don't have to if you don't want to, Charlie. It's just an idea."

A wide, gap-toothed grin spread slowly across Charlie's face. "Of course I'll mail it for you, Poppy. It's a brilliant idea! And I'm sure that private investigator will have a lovely time looking for you all over Ribbleswold!"

Later, when Charlie had gone home and Marie Claire was sitting in the kitchen with Poppy, sampling the raspberry jam shortbreads, she pushed an old photo album across the table. "I thought you might like to look through this, *chérie*. Mmmmm, by the way, these are superb!" Marie Claire said, kissing the fingertips of her left hand. "Maybe a touch more vanilla, *n'est-ce pas*?"

"Yes, you're right," Poppy agreed, opening the

leather cover of the photo album and breathing in an old-fashioned smell of dust and lavender water. "Who is that?" she said, staring at a black-and-white picture of a sad-looking young girl. The girl was dressed in a tartan school uniform and had a beret perched on top of her tightly braided hair.

"That's me," Marie Claire murmured. "Before I ran away to Paris."

"You ran away?" Poppy looked up, startled.

"I was brought up in an orphanage in Bordeaux," Marie Claire explained. "My parents were both lost in a boating accident, you see, so I was put in the orphanage because there was no one else to take me. It was an awful experience, and the food—" Marie Claire wrinkled up her nose. "It was unbearable." She leaned over and lightly touched a finger to the photograph. "We were all sent to a strict school where the teachers beat us for everything, even smiling. No one listened to us or cared about our dreams."

"How terrible."

"It was, *chérie*, and I couldn't wait to get away, so one night, when everyone was sleeping, I packed my bags and left. Hitched a ride all the way to Paris."

"What did you do when you got there?"

"Like you, I found a job working in a bakery. It was the smell that enticed me. I had never experienced anything like it, certainly not in the orphanage, which always stank of wet socks and boiled cabbage. The bread they used to give us was so stale and dry it scratched your mouth when you ate it. And it had no smell. But standing outside that patisserie in Paris . . ." Marie Claire breathed deeply as if she could still sniff the long-ago air. "The scent was intoxicating. I stood there all morning, smelling fresh bread baking and feeling like I had come home." She paused for a moment, studying the photograph, and then glanced up at Poppy thoughtfully. "When I finally gathered enough courage to go inside, the owner gave me a job washing pans. I didn't mind though," Marie Claire remarked. "Just like you, *chérie*, I got to spend all my time in the kitchen, surrounded by those wonderful scents."

"That makes us sort of the same," Poppy said, smiling at Marie Claire.

"Except you have parents and I didn't," Marie Claire pointed out in a quiet voice. She flipped over the page to show an elderly gentleman in a long white apron. "That's Monsieur Claude," Marie Claire said fondly. "He owned the bakery where I worked, and what a genius the man was. It was Monsieur Claude who showed me how to take flour and water and turn them into something magical." Marie Claire gave a long, soulful sigh. "Even today I cannot make a baguette to rival Monsieur Claude's. Warm hands and a warm heart, that's the key, he used to say."

Poppy picked at a piece of dry cookie dough that was stuck to the top of the table. "I don't understand why you're showing me this," she said, not meeting Marie Claire's gaze.

"Perhaps," Marie Claire spoke carefully, "perhaps because I noticed a sadness in your face when you first arrived. Something that reminded me of myself all those years ago. Like you said, Poppy, we are sort of the same."

Poppy wished she could tell Marie Claire the truth. It would feel so good to let out all the words crammed up inside her. To explain what it had been like living at home with the shadow of Great-Granny Mabel always hovering overhead. To admit how much she hated magic and how awful Ruthersfield was. How her parents didn't like it when she made cookie batter instead of spells, and worst of all, how they had banned her from ever seeing Charlie again. Poppy sighed, opening her mouth, but no words would come. She didn't want to tell too much. After all, Marie Claire was a grown-up, and even though she wanted to help, if she knew the truth, she might feel obliged to send Poppy back home. "Well, I won't go," Poppy whispered, biting into a raspberry jam shortbread. "I'm never leaving here," she added fiercely, speaking louder than she'd intended.

"Poppy," Marie Claire began, but Poppy covered her ears.

"I don't want to talk about me, Marie Claire. Please, not right now."

"Your parents know you are safe, which is good, but I need to talk to them. You did write yesterday, *chérie*?"

"I did," Poppy said, wishing Marie Claire would stop staring at her. "But I only posted the letter today," she confessed. "Please don't be cross with me."

Marie Claire didn't answer. She just took one of Poppy's hands in her own and squeezed it hard.

Chapter Eleven

A Glimpse Through the Window

POPPY COULDN'T BELIEVE HOW PERFECT HER LIFE HAD become. Charlie spent Friday, after school, and most of her weekend at the bakery, skipping home only for meals. Usually when she arrived at Marie Claire's, she would find Poppy busy in the kitchen, cooking. In fact, Poppy had hardly left the kitchen, because she was so scared of being seen. Charlie liked to pull up a stool next to the big butcher-block table and watch as Poppy mixed and stirred, kneading bread dough or dolloping out cookie batter. They listened to the loud French music Marie Claire loved, gradually learning the words and singing along, even though they didn't know what they were singing about. It didn't matter. The girls were happy, and Marie Claire could hear them giggling away as she stood in the shop, serving customers.

If Poppy needed one of the rare, special ingredients that Marie Claire kept on the highest shelves in the kitchen, she entertained Charlie by jumping up like a jack-in-the-box to reach them. Marie Claire did keep a stepladder handy for just such a purpose, but Poppy ignored it, springing eight feet through the air and grabbing fresh vanilla beans or French chocolate off the shelves. This was fun to watch but not always successful, and Charlie found herself showered in macaroons when Poppy accidentally knocked a box of them over as she reached for the vanilla!

"Poppy," Marie Claire said gently, after Charlie had left on Sunday. "There has been no word yet from your parents. If we have not heard back by tomorrow evening, I must contact them myself."

"No, please don't. Oh, please don't," Poppy begged, staring at Marie Claire out of frightened eyes.

Bending down, Marie Claire brushed a loose strand of hair out of Poppy's face. "I have to, *chérie*. We will face this together. Everything will be all right. I promise."

"No, it won't. They'll make me go back to Ruthersfield," Poppy said in a wobbly voice. "And I don't want to leave here."

"I'm sorry, Poppy, but I have no choice."

Poppy saw that Marie Claire was serious. There was no avoiding this problem any longer. "Can you talk to my dad, then?" Poppy whispered. "He might understand better than my mum."

Marie Claire gave Poppy a hug. "Of course I will, *chérie*. Now try not to worry any more tonight."

Early the following morning, before the store opened, Poppy risked helping Marie Claire carry out loaves of walnut bread from the kitchen. As she pushed through the swinging door, her arms full of warm bread, Poppy caught a glimpse of Auntie Viv, walking past the patisserie. At least it looked like her auntie Viv, same orange hair and large, expansive bottom, but she was gone before Poppy could be absolutely sure. What made her heart start to thump and her legs go all trembly was the way the woman had hesitated a second as she glanced through the window. It hadn't been more than the briefest of moments, a quick turn of the head, but Poppy felt queasy as she arranged the loaves of bread on a shelf. Had it been Auntie Viv, and if so, had she seen Poppy?

Was she marching over to the Pendles' house right this very instant to tell them where their daughter was hiding? Poppy groaned.

"Are you all right, *chérie*?" Marie Claire inquired, coming up behind her with a tray of almond croissants. Poppy had her arms wrapped tightly around her stomach and was rocking to and fro.

"I feel a bit sick," she whispered, staring at the window. "I don't feel good at all."

"Go and lie down," Marie Claire suggested. "You've gone all pale."

"I think I will," Poppy said. "I think I might be about to faint." She hurried back into the kitchen and collapsed on her little camp bed, fear and worry knotting her stomach into tight cramps. She knew she was going to have to face her parents at some point soon, probably talk to them tonight when Marie Claire called, but this wasn't how she wanted it to happen. Marie Claire tiptoed in and out, checking on Poppy between customers, and as the morning slipped by without any sign of her parents turning up, Poppy began to calm down. She must have been mistaken. It couldn't have been Auntie Viv at all, or if it had been Auntie Viv, she obviously hadn't seen Poppy. Still, a nagging doubt continued to trouble her, and she couldn't stop her mind from replaying the moment over and over again. It was impossible to switch her thoughts off, so Poppy did what she always did whenever she was feeling upset. She baked. Buttery coffee cupcakes soon filled the kitchen with their comforting, homey smell, and by the time Charlie arrived, Poppy had almost convinced herself that she had spent most of the day worrying about nothing.

"Marie Claire told me you weren't feeling too well," Charlie said, hesitating in the doorway. "Should I go so you can rest?"

"No, no, I'm fine, really. Just a headache, but it's gone now." Poppy smiled, not wanting her friend to leave. "Let's do something fun," she suggested, trying to make things seem normal. "We can take cupcakes outside and play basketball. Although I should probably help tidy up the shop first," Poppy said. "I haven't been much use today."

"I thought you didn't like going out front," Charlie said.

"Well, I don't usually, but I hate Marie Claire having to do everything by herself."

"I'll help," Charlie offered, grabbing a broom. "I don't mind sweeping."

As Poppy followed Charlie out of the kitchen, she tried to ignore the sense of uneasiness that wouldn't, however much she wanted it to, quite go away.

....

Chapter Twelve

Back Home

AFTER MAKING SURE THAT THE CLOSED SIGN WAS UP and the door locked, Poppy started to wipe down the counter. It had been a busy day and there was nothing left in the display case except for a single misshapen croissant. Marie Claire was singing softly to herself, one of her favorite French songs, and Poppy and Charlie had just joined in when there came a sudden pounding of fists on the front door. It sounded like a hailstorm smacking against the glass. Poppy froze, gripping her dust cloth and staring at the clenched-up fist banging on the door. She couldn't move, and when the knocking got so aggressive it was clear that the glass might break, Marie Claire walked slowly toward it.

"No, please," Poppy begged. "Don't!" But Marie Claire was already sliding back the bolt. Before she had even removed her hand, the door was shoved open and Edith and Roger Pendle burst into the shop.

"Poppy," Edith Pendle cried out, her pale face crumpling like a squashed dinner roll. "Are you all right, sweetheart? Has she hurt you?" she sobbed, hurrying over and pulling Poppy hard against her. Poppy didn't answer, but her eyes filled with tears as she stood there being hugged by her mother. Marie Claire was staring at the Pendles in astonishment. You couldn't mistake Roger and Edith Pendle, not even after ten whole years. She had wondered for so long about the baby born in her shop that distant May afternoon, and now it all made perfect sense. Of course Poppy was that baby, and even though the air was thick with unpleasantness, Marie Claire found herself smiling.

"We should have known you were behind this," Edith Pendle accused Marie Claire, shaking with anger as she held Poppy close. "You, of all people. I hold you fully responsible. You stole our child." She wept. "Making us think she had run off to Ribbleswold. It's you who's been filling her brain with all this cooking nonsense, isn't it? From the very beginning you've been planning this, haven't you, just because, just because . . ." But Edith Pendle couldn't finish. She started to heave with fresh tears, hugging Poppy so tightly it was difficult for the girl to breathe.

"You think you have some sort of a special claim on my daughter," Roger Pendle said. "Well, I'm — I'm tempted to call the police and press kidnapping charges."

"NO!" Poppy burst out, pushing her mother away. "No, please don't. Marie Claire didn't kidnap me. I came here on my own. This has nothing to do with her."

"Oh, my poor lamb," Mrs. Pendle said. "You've been brainwashed, as well. Come on, sweetheart, we're taking you home."

"No, please." Poppy panicked, looking pleadingly at Marie Claire. "Don't let them take me. I don't want to go."

"Of course you do," her mother crooned, gripping Poppy's arm and tugging her toward the door.

"No, please, I'm begging you, let me stay here." Poppy's voice wobbled with hysteria.

"Come on, Poppy," Roger Pendle coaxed, shuffling about in discomfort. "This isn't where you live, pumpkin. You need to come home."

"Can't you do something?" Charlie cried, turning to Marie Claire for help. "You mustn't let them take her."

"So you're involved in this too, are you?" Edith

Pendle said, pointing at Charlie. "See what I mean, Roger? A bad influence."

"I'm sorry." Marie Claire shook her head sadly. "There is nothing I can do. You have to go with your parents, Poppy. And I'm sorry you have been so worried," Marie Claire said, addressing the Pendles. "Did you not get Poppy's letter?"

"Oh, we got it all right," Edith Pendle said. "Filled with a lot of nonsense."

"It's not your fault. I didn't tell them where I was," Poppy confessed, looking at Marie Claire. "Because I knew this would happen."

"Oh, I hate this place," Poppy's mother sobbed. "Always have done, right from the very beginning. All I ever wanted was a nice hospital bed for the delivery, just like every other woman in Potts Bottom."

"It's all right, Edith," Roger Pendle murmured, putting his arm around his wife and handing her a handkerchief.

"No, it's not all right, it's not. I never want to see this awful bakery again." Edith Pendle blew her nose. "And did you tell her, did you?" She seethed, glaring at Marie Claire. Poor Poppy had no idea what her parents were talking about, and she looked helplessly over at Marie Claire.

"It is not my job to tell Poppy that marvelous story;

it's yours. But you should," Marie Claire said. "We all need to know our beginnings. Poppy is a wonderful cook," she continued. "There are not many young girls who have such a passion and a talent for baking. You should be proud of her," she finished bravely, her voice starting to quiver. "It has been a real pleasure getting to know your magnificent daughter."

"Proud of her," Roger Pendle spluttered. "We're proud of her, all right. She's top in her class at Ruthersfield Academy."

"That's right," Edith Pendle said. Her jaw trembled with emotion as she spoke. "My daughter has been blessed with the gift of magic, and nobody, nobody is going to take that away from her, especially you."

"I wouldn't dream—" Marie Claire began, but Mrs. Pendle had already yanked open the patisserie door and was pulling Poppy outside.

"Wait." Charlie raced after them. "Can I at least say good-bye?"

"No, you can't," Edith Pendle fumed as she hustled Poppy into the back of a waiting car. "And if I ever find you communicating with my daughter again, I'll have you arrested for, for, for interference with a witch."

All the strength had seeped out of Poppy's body, and she slumped on the car's backseat like a rag doll. Charlie was knocking against the window, but Poppy turned her head away and covered her face with her hands.

"I thought it was you this morning," a familiar voice said, and peeking through her fingers, Poppy saw Auntie Viv sitting beside her. "Scaring your parents half to death like that," she tutted, leaning over to plant a kiss on Poppy's cheek. "Still, we're just glad you're okay, aren't we? Home safe now, sweetheart." Poppy didn't answer. She wrapped her arms around her knees and dropped her head forward, wishing she could disappear.

Chapter Thirteen

A Fresh Coat of Paint and a New Wand

WHEN THE PENDLE FAMILY ARRIVED HOME, MAXINE from next door was waiting in front of their house. As Poppy got out of the car, Maxine trotted right over. "So glad you're safe, lovey. We've all been worried sick about you."

"She's fine, she's fine," Edith Pendle said, putting her arm around Poppy. "Roger wants to press kidnapping charges."

"Kidnapped, ohhh!" Maxine shivered with the thrill of such juicy news. "Never, Edith, really?"

"Kidnapped, brainwashed. It's been a nightmare, honestly." Edith Pendle squeezed her daughter. "We're just so pleased to have Poppy home again, so if you'll excuse us, I'm going to tuck her up in bed."

"A good night's sleep," Maxine called after them. "She'll be right as rain."

Poppy let her mother lead her into the house, her father and Auntie Viv following behind. "Now, you're not to worry about a thing," Edith Pendle said, hustling Poppy up the stairs. "You'll make up the work you've missed in no time, and just look at this room," she chattered on. "Surprise, surprise!" Poppy stared at her bedroom in dismay. Her Young Chef of the Year poster had been taken down, and so had the framed photographs of cakes and breads she had bought with her birthday money last May. In their place were posters of famous witches, highlighting the spectacular achievements they had each accomplished. And this was not all. The walls were no longer yellow. Instead they had been painted a purplish-plum color, and the picture of Great-Granny Mabel that had always sat on the hall table was now perched on top of her bureau. Stars and moons had been stenciled all over the ceiling, and a new handwoven rug with the Ruthersfield crest on it was spread out beside the bed.

"Where are my things?" Poppy asked in shock, noticing that her bookshelf of cookbooks had all been replaced with magical study guides.

"This room hasn't been redecorated in years," Edith Pendle said cheerily. "And it's completely our fault. I've been reading all about it. A good study environment is essential to young witches. It took us the whole weekend." She smiled at Poppy. "Now I'll bring you up some soup, lamb."

"And did you notice your new magic wand?" Roger Pendle asked his daughter. He pointed to a shiny black wand, tied around with a purple ribbon, that was sitting next to Great-Granny Mabel's picture. "It's the latest model," he said proudly. "Very sensitive, that is. Ms. Roach only recommends them for her star pupils."

Sinking down on her bed, Poppy surveyed the room in silence.

"Well, go on, Roger," Edith Pendle hissed. "This is a good time. Talk to her."

"So, Poppy," Mr. Pendle began, walking over to his daughter. He cleared his throat and glanced at his wife.

"Say it," Edith Pendle instructed. "You're her father."

"We do need to talk about the fact that you ran away," Mr. Pendle said, hovering next to Poppy. "We were worried sick." He pulled a handkerchief out of his pocket and dabbed it over his forehead. "I was worried sick."

"Taking off like that in the middle of the night. In

the middle of our favorite show," Mrs. Pendle added.

"You knew I was safe," Poppy whispered. "I called you. And I wrote you a letter explaining."

"Not an ounce of consideration for our feelings," her mother continued. "Honestly, Poppy. Why would you do such a thing? I was out of my mind with worry. And having to lie to the school like I did and tell them you were sick." Edith Pendle took a long, deep breath and closed her eyes for a moment. "We won't talk about it anymore, though. Daddy and I love you, but you just need to know how much you scared us."

"Did you even read my letter?" Poppy said, looking up at her mother.

"I did, and I forgive you, sweetheart." Edith gave a quivery smile. "We all say things we don't mean when we're under stress, but everything's going to be fine now. Come on, Roger," she clucked. "Poppy's exhausted, poor thing. Look at her sitting there, all pale and droopy."

"What did Marie Claire mean when she said everyone needs to know about their beginnings?" Poppy asked in a small voice. "What marvelous story should you tell me about?" Her mother's mouth narrowed into a tight line.

"I'll be right back with your soup," she replied. "That's just what you need."

Alone in her bedroom at last, Poppy realized that it wasn't just the walls and ceiling her parents had redecorated. They had also put up some new window treatments especially for her return. Covering the pane of glass were thick iron bars that broke up the sunlight and made opening the window impossible.

When her mother tiptoed in with a bowl of lukewarm canned soup, Poppy pretended to be asleep. She had crawled under the covers in her clothes, not bothering to put on pajamas, wash her face, or brush her teeth. "I'll leave this here in case you want it later," Edith Pendle whispered, putting the bowl down and tugging new purple velvet curtains across the iron bars. "Now sleep tight, sweetheart. We're so glad you're back home. Get a good night's rest because it's school tomorrow." And as her mother left the room, Poppy heard the click of a key turning shut. So even if she wanted to run away again, it would be impossible to escape from this fancy purple prison.

In the morning Poppy woke early. She was used to getting up at four to start the bread doughs and croissants, and even though she wasn't at the bakery anymore, Poppy still got out of bed. She decided to go downstairs and make some orange currant scones. Her parents could take her away from Marie Claire's, but they couldn't stop her from baking. Except that Poppy had forgotten about the door. It wouldn't open when she turned the handle, and only then did she remember that her mother had locked her in. It was seven o'clock before she heard her father fumbling about with the key, and as soon as Mr. Pendle opened the door, Poppy raced past him and down the stairs. He immediately dashed after her.

"Don't worry," Poppy called over her shoulder. "I'm only going to the kitchen. I thought I'd make scones for breakfast." But to her horror she discovered that the oven had disappeared. There was a gaping hole in the middle of the counter where the stove had once been.

"Your mother didn't think we needed it anymore," Roger Pendle said sheepishly. "She thought it was a distraction for you."

"A distraction." Poppy stared at the hole. "It's an oven."

"That's right," Edith Pendle agreed, bustling into the kitchen. "But it kept you away from your studies, Poppy. All that baking when you should have been practicing your magic," she said. "I thought it would be simpler for you not to have it around. You know, take away the temptation. We can easily put it back in later, after you graduate. And anyway," she finished, "I hardly ever used it myself. The microwave is all we really need."

"I used that oven though," Poppy said in a small, tight voice. "I used it all the time. I liked that oven," she whispered, starting to tremble with pent-up anger. "You took away the one thing in this house that made me happy."

"Oh, now, don't exaggerate," Edith Pendle said, opening the freezer and taking out a box of toaster tarts. She ripped the top off and shook three of them into the microwave. "You've no idea how lucky you are, Poppy, honestly. This program I watched last night said that fewer and fewer girls are being born with the gift of magic. Only one in fifteen thousand, according to the latest research, and most of those have only a fraction of your powers."

"I don't want to be a witch," Poppy shouted, shaking with emotion. She could smell the chemical sweetness of heating toaster tarts.

"Listen, Poppy, your father and I support you one hundred percent," Edith Pendle said, speaking slowly to emphasize the seriousness of her words. "Truly, we do. Right now you have no idea what's best for you, but one day you will. One day you'll thank us for doing the right thing."

"Like taking away the oven," Poppy cried, "and making me come back here when I loved living with Marie Claire and cooking every day?"

Roger Pendle cleared his throat. "Well, that's right," he added, although he didn't sound quite as convinced as his wife. He tweaked one of Poppy's braids affectionately.

"Have a toaster tart," Mrs. Pendle offered, holding out a steaming square of something that looked to be made out of cardboard. Poppy waved her mother's hand away, and a stream of tiny bunched up silver fists flowed from her fingers into the air.

"Oh, that's so clever," Edith Pendle exclaimed. "You have such talent, sweetheart." One of the miniature fists smacked the toaster tart she was holding onto the floor, and another one punched her right in the nose.

Poppy refused to go to school. "I've got a really bad headache," she told her parents, which happened to be the truth. The horrible smell of toaster tarts wasn't helping either, and Poppy thought she might be sick.

"You can't do this." Mrs. Pendle fretted, following her daughter upstairs to bed. Poppy buried herself under the covers and curled up into a tight ball. "You've already missed four days of lessons," Edith Pendle pointed out.

"Mum, I don't feel good," Poppy whispered into her pillow. "Please let me sleep."

"I cannot believe you are doing this to me," her mother muttered. "This is so unfair, Poppy."

"Oh, Edith, give her the day in bed," Mr. Pendle whispered, shuffling into Poppy's room behind them. "She doesn't look well."

"Fine." Edith Pendle sighed, and then lowering her voice, she added, "Although I've just about had enough of this nonsense." She drew the curtains shut and turned out the light. "Sleep it off, Poppy, because tomorrow, no more excuses."

·····························

Chapter Fourteen

The Stop It Now Spell

THE FOLLOWING MORNING MR. AND MRS. PENDLE insisted on driving Poppy to Ruthersfield. Of course they didn't trust her to fly, Poppy realized, not that she had anywhere left to fly to. She couldn't go back to Marie Claire's.

"We'll pick you up after school," Edith Pendle announced in the car, as if this was just another regular day. "I told Auntie Viv that after we've done our home- work, we'll all go to dinner at that new MockTurdles Burger Palace." She turned around and smiled at Poppy as Roger Pendle pulled to a stop in front of Ruthersfield. "Now, hurry on in, you don't want to be late." Leaning across the front seat, she straightened the collar of Poppy's blouse. "We called Ms. Roach last night and she's expecting you. She thinks you've been down with a nasty case of tonsillitis." Edith Pendle's lips tightened and her smile disappeared. "According to Ms. Roach, most Ruthersfield girls never miss school. She was extremely understanding, Poppy. You should be grateful."

If Poppy had thought her first day at the academy had been bad, getting out in front of all these gawking girls was far, far worse. She had only been gone from school for five days, but clearly it was enough time for the girls to find something to gossip about. Poppy could hear them whispering her name behind their hands, and she hung her head as she slipped through the crowd, dragging her broomstick behind her. Ms. Roach was standing at the front door, greeting the girls as they trickled in. "Hope you're feeling better, Poppy," the headmistress said, giving her a practiced smile. It was as if the past wonderful week had never happened, as if by pretending she had been sick with tonsillitis, her time at Marie Claire's could somehow be wiped out. It was the Edith and Roger approach, Poppy decided. It was the "let's ignore the fact that our daughter just ran away and spent the happiest week of her life cooking in a bakery" approach. Not that it mattered anymore,

Poppy thought as she slumped along the corridor. Nothing mattered now. She couldn't even bake at home. There was no oven left to cook in!

A cloud as dark and black as brewing thunder settled over Poppy's head. It hovered above her as she walked into her spells and charms honors class, and when she sat down, the cloud draped itself around her like a cloak.

"Aha," Miss Weedle said, looking right at Poppy. "I can see that someone is not in the best of moods this morning." Again Poppy didn't speak. She had run out of words. There was nothing left to say. So she just stared at Miss Weedle. "Well, you should do extremely well with our new spell today, Poppy. It requires a good deal of forceful energy behind it," Miss Weedle said, punching the air with her fist and writing "Stop It Now," across the blackboard in large, bold letters. "This spell," she explained in a serious voice, "is powerful, really powerful, and must only be used in special circumstances. You girls are not to fool about with it."

"What sort of special circumstances?" Megan Roberts piped up.

"Like stopping something harmful from happening, something big. For example," Miss Weedle told the class, "if you saw a car speeding out of control and about to hit a person, well, then you could cast the Stop

It Now Spell. It would stop the car in its tracks and prevent an accident from occurring."

"Wow." Megan Roberts looked awestruck. So did the rest of the girls. Only Poppy seemed lost in her own thoughts.

"This spell has many uses," Miss Weedle continued. "Five years ago Margaret Clark, one of our most famous alumnae and a well-respected scientist, used it to stop a meteorite from hitting the planet Earth. She received a Noblet Prize for her quick thinking."

"So that's what it does. It stops things?" Fanny Freeman confirmed, rapidly taking notes.

"Well, there are subtle variations to the Stop It Now Spell," Miss Weedle said. "Stopping a fast-moving object is using the spell in its simplest form, but it can also turn the object in question to stone. Now that," Miss Weedle cautioned in a grave voice, "that is much more complex. It requires a great deal of forceful energy to produce such an effect. Pent-up anger or bottled aggression work very well as a catalyst for this type of spell. So since you seem to be full of the grumps this morning, Poppy, why don't you come up here and give it a try?" Poppy pushed back her chair and walked between the rows of desks. She stumbled over Megan's book bag, managing to get one of the long leather straps caught around her shoe. As she bent down to untangle it, a smattering of giggles burst out. Megan whispered "clunterpoke" under her breath, but Poppy didn't seem to hear. She just shuffled on to the front of the class and stood there, clutching her new magic wand.

A cage had been set up on the floor with a little white mouse in it. "Now, when I give the command," Miss Weedle told Poppy, "I shall open this cage door and let the mouse free. Over there," she instructed, pointing to the far corner of the room, "is a wedge of vintage cheddar. This particular breed of mouse has a highly developed sense of smell, so it will, I'm hoping, dash toward the cheese at high speed. Your job, Poppy, is to stop it. Point your wand at the mouse and harness those emotions you seem to be harboring this morning. Then simply say the word"—and here Miss Weedle breathed in deeply, before exhaling with a dramatic— "Consticrabihaltus."

"Consticrabihaltus," Poppy copied.

"More feeling, Poppy. You need raw emotion behind this spell to make it work. Now, are you ready?" Miss Weedle asked. Poppy nodded and blinked back tears. She honestly couldn't believe she was back here at Ruthersfield again, away from the warmth and comfort of Marie Claire's kitchen. Who would make the caramel cookies today, she wondered, and how could her parents do this to her?

"Ready, then? One, two, three," Miss Weedle said, and with a flip of the latch, she opened the cage door. Immediately the tiny mouse started to scurry across the floor toward the cheddar. With a wave of her wand, Poppy yelled out furiously, "Consticrabihaltus." The mouse froze about two feet from the cheese, its little pink tongue peeping through a set of sharp, pointy teeth.

"Magnificent," Miss Weedle cried out. "Oh, I couldn't have done that better myself. You can practice this for homework, girls. Don't use a live creature though, please. Undoing a spell like this is rather complex. Just roll a ball across the floor and try to stop it. There's a box of rubber balls by the door, so take one on your way out. Now open up those spell books to page forty-six."

The rest of the morning dragged on endlessly. Poppy suffered through foreign history (they were studying different types of witchcraft in other countries), followed by music and the art of spell chanting.

"So where've you been?" Megan Roberts asked Poppy at lunch. "I'll bet you weren't really sick. I'll bet you ran away." She was spooning up custard, exchanging knowing glances with her friends.

"I did," Poppy said, hunching forward under her cloak of misery.

"Well, you'll have tons of extra work. Five days of school is a lot to miss. It's been really hard lately, but I got As on the last three tests so I'm top of the class at the moment." Megan shook back her hair. "You'll probably have to do weekend makeup classes, I should imagine."

"No, I won't," Poppy said, wanting to shock the smug expression off Megan's face. She slammed down her ham sandwich and shouted, "I hate it here. I hate being a witch. I ran off and joined a bakery, if you must know." There was a collective gasp from around the table, and Megan made the sign of a sickle moon.

"How can you say such a thing?" she questioned. "We're the lucky ones. Everyone wants to be able to do magic."

"Not me," Poppy said simply, feeling her anger seep away. Tears clouded her eyes. "I just want to be able to bake."

"You're so odd," Megan sneered, picking up her bowl of custard and moving over to another table. All the other girls followed and Poppy was left sitting alone.

When the bell rang at the end of the last lesson, Poppy found Charlie waiting for her outside the school gates. "Don't worry," Charlie reassured her at once. "Your parents didn't see me. I managed to sneak by them. They're parked out front."

"What are you doing here?" Poppy worried. "I don't want to get you into trouble, Charlie, and if my mum catches you talking to me . . ."

"Oh, I had to see you," Charlie spoke in a rush. "After what happened, I just had to see you. I can't believe how, how . . ."

"How much my parents want me to be a witch?" Poppy finished. "Oh, you've no idea, Charlie."

"Poor Marie Claire feels awful," Charlie said. "She was so upset after you'd gone. I stayed to help finish cleaning up, and she just kept sweeping the same patch of floor over and over again, muttering away about babies and fate. I don't know what she was talking about, but she looked so sad."

"I wish she could have kept me," Poppy whispered in a quivery voice, tears dripping down her face. "She was so kind to me. Now I'll probably never see her again."

"Oh, no, you will. You have to," Charlie said in anguish. "She's desperate to see you. Maybe in a week or so when things have calmed down a bit?"

"Things will never calm down with my parents," Poppy said, wiping a hand across her eyes. "They took out the oven in our house so I can't bake anymore."

As if on cue, Edith Pendle could be seen clipping up the wide front stairs, a determined look on her face. Charlie quickly pushed her way into the middle of a crowd of girls, and was swept out of sight.

"There you are, sweetheart," Poppy's mother said. "Daddy and I have been waiting for you out front."

"I can fly home, you know," Poppy murmured, uncomfortable with all the attention.

"Of course you can, Poppy. We just wanted to come and meet you. See how school went." Edith Pendle linked her arm through her daughter's. "So how was it today?" she questioned. "Are you behind in your subjects? Do you have a lot of homework?"

"A bit," Poppy sighed, trying to pull her arm free. She could see Megan and some of the other girls snickering as they walked by. Poppy moved slowly, as if her sadness was weighing her down. She felt a wave of despair crash over her, washing away any last sense of hope and leaving her hollow inside.

Chapter Fifteen

....

The Dark Side

BACK HOME, MRS. PENDLE PRODUCED A BOX OF Twirlies for a snack—chemical-tasting sponge cake bars filled with fake cream—and poured out three large glasses of Super Savers cola.

"What time are we meeting Viv for dinner?" Mr. Pendle asked his wife. "Because there's a show on television later about tracing your magical roots back to the Vikings. Might be fun."

"I said I'd call her when Poppy's finished her homework," Mrs. Pendle said, biting off a chunk of Twirlie bar. "We're not going anywhere till that's done," she added firmly. "Homework first, and it looks like there's plenty of it tonight, right, Poppy?" Edith Pendle sat down at the table next to her daughter and frowned at the pile of books. "You've got a lot to do, sweetie." Poppy was halfway through a paper on wand technique. She bit her lip in frustration, trying to ignore her mother. Mrs. Pendle reached out a hand and picked up Poppy's creative magic journal. The girls were required to keep track of any new spell ideas and spontaneous magical moments that happened to them throughout the day.

"Mum, please, that's private," Poppy snapped, grabbing it back and inadvertently knocking over her untouched glass of cola. It flooded the table, drenching textbooks and papers and running onto the floor in a sticky brown pool.

"Your homework!" Mrs. Pendle wailed, frantically shoving books aside and trying to stem the flow of soda with her cardigan. "What a mess, what a mess. Now you'll have to redo it all. Roger, throw me a sponge, quick." She turned on her daughter in frustration. "Well, help out, Poppy." But Poppy didn't move. "Oh, look at this, it's ruined, it's just ruined," Mrs. Pendle screeched, trying to peel the paper on wand technique off the table. "Come on, Poppy, don't just sit there." Tears filled Mrs. Pendle's eyes and she started to sob quietly. "Honestly, I don't know what to do with you.

You fight us on everything. You have opportunities most girls only dream about, and you're throwing them all away. We've done everything for you," she cried. "We've supported you. We've always been there for you, and I know it's not about the money," she sniffed, "but the sacrifices we've made." Her voice wobbled with emotion, and Poppy covered her ears.

"Mum, stop it. Please."

"No, I won't stop it. Do you have any idea, Poppy, how our lives revolve around you? And then running away like that." Edith Pendle blew her nose loudly. "I can't pretend I wasn't hurt." She stared at her daughter in silence, breathing shakily.

"You don't understand," Poppy said at last, her lips trembling. "You don't care about what I want at all," Poppy added, bursting into tears.

"I know best. You are only a child," Mrs. Pendle said, aghast. "How can you say that?"

"Because you never hear me," Poppy shouted. "You don't listen, Mum, ever. It's you that wants me to be a witch," she sobbed, shoving her chair back from the table. "I don't. I never have. I hate magic. I just want to bake cakes."

"Ah!" Edith Pendle put a hand over her heart as if she were in severe pain. "Thank goodness Great-Granny Mabel isn't here. She'd be mortified if she heard you speaking that way. Isn't that right, Roger?"

Mr. Pendle nodded, fiddling with the buttons on his cardigan. "She'd be heartbroken," he agreed. "You've been given a marvelous gift, Poppy, love, and we can't bear to see you wasting it like this."

"Just leave me alone," Poppy yelled, her sadness overtaken by a growing wave of anger. "Leave. Me. Alone."

"You've let the family down, Poppy," Edith Pendle hissed. "That's what you've done. Let us all down."

"Now, take it easy, Edith," Roger Pendle said, shuffling over to her in his slippers.

Edith Pendle took a couple of deep breaths, steadying herself on her husband's arm. In a more composed voice she said, "We need to get this mess cleared up so Poppy can get on with her homework."

Poppy sat quite still, the anger inside her swelling. There was a long, drawn-out silence, except for the sound of Mrs. Pendle's heavy breathing as she unwrapped a Twirlie bar and took a big bite. Then leaning forward, Poppy shoved her spell book onto the floor, where it landed in a puddle of sticky cola. "NO!" She glared at her mother in defiance. "I will not."

"Now, come on, Poppy," Roger Pendle said, folding his arms across his chest in a show of authority. "Do as your mother asks, please. Finish up your homework."

Mrs. Pendle's long face was full of self-pity, and she looked tearfully at her daughter as she chewed.

"All right," Poppy agreed huskily, pulling her magic wand out of her backpack with hands that were shaking almost as much as her voice. "I'll do my homework if that's what you want. This is a new spell I learned in school today and I have to practice it," she sobbed, waving the wand at her parents. "CONSTICRABIHALTUS," Poppy shouted, firing out the words with so much fury that Mrs. Pendle had not only stopped crying but was rapidly beginning to turn the color of a lead pencil. So was Mr. Pendle, who stood motionless beside his wife, a startled look plastered across his face.

For an hour or more, Poppy sat at the table, too horrified to move, as she watched her parents turn to stone. First their arms and legs and faces, then their hair, and finally even the clothes they wore. It was weird, watching the color leach away from her mother's orange sweater, seeing how her skirt hung in stony folds so that she looked as if she had been carved from a piece of solid granite by a master craftsman. All she could think about was Madeline Reynolds. Did she feel like this too when she had washed away half of Italy? Despair and shame flooded Poppy, and she was filled with a heavy sense of guilt. This wasn't at all what she had intended. She had only wanted to stop them from going on at her, shut them up for a bit. Now the house was so quiet Poppy could hear the drip, drip, drip of the kitchen tap. When the phone started to ring, it sounded as loud and invasive as a fire alarm. Poppy sat and listened to it blare on and on. Finally the answering machine picked up and Auntie Viv's voice could be heard, yabbering away into the silent room.

Another hour passed, and still Poppy didn't move. She wondered if her heart had also turned to stone, because it sat inside her chest as cold and heavy as a boulder. Finally Poppy pushed back her chair and walked over to where her parents stood. Mrs. Pendle's face was as long and mournful as a bloodhound's, tragedy fossilized into every line. Poppy reached out a hand, touching the stone cheek that still bulged with Twirlie bar. She knocked against it gently with her knuckles. It was hard and unforgiving. Her father stood with his arms folded across his chest, his stone feet encased in a pair of stone slippers.

Miss Weedle had been right about the Stop It Now Spell. It was shockingly powerful and Poppy had mastered it perfectly. Ironically, her mother would have been delighted by such an accomplishment, had she been available for comment. Anger started to swell up in Poppy again. *I'll bet nobody else in the class managed to turn their rubber balls into stone,* Poppy thought, shoving three boxes of Twirlies and some cans of meat stew into her backpack. Who cared what she ate now? "I hope you're happy, Edith," Poppy challenged, addressing the statue-like Mrs. Pendle. She stuck her wand on top of the Twirlies. "Because this is what you wanted, isn't it, Mum? I'm an excellent witch," she said, "just like Great-Granny Mabel. And I'll never bake again either. You don't need to worry about that. There's no oven here, and I'm not going back to Marie Claire's." If anyone knew what she had done to her parents, they'd be horrified, and Poppy couldn't bear Marie Claire's disappointment. Even if she wanted to, she had no idea how to change her parents back again. Right now she felt hopeless. When the police found out what she had done, they would take her off to Scrubs Prison and lock her up. Poppy was sure of that. But her anger and sadness were so deep she didn't care. She didn't care about anything anymore. Shouldering her backpack, Poppy looked at her mother one last time and gave a hard laugh. "You've got what you wished for, Mum. I'm a witch all right."

Leaving her parents standing in the kitchen, Poppy grabbed her broomstick and left through the front door. She wasn't running away this time. She had nothing to run from and nowhere to run to. Noticing Maxine's cat stalking across the top of the garden fence, Poppy whipped out her wand, and with an aggressive wave of her hand, she turned it straight into stone.

It was five o'clock on a Wednesday evening, and Poppy Pendle had passed over to the dark side.

Chapter Sixteen

....

Poppy Pendle Disappears

AS POPPY TRUDGED INTO POTTS BOTTOM, SHE scowled at a row of little blackbirds chirping away on a telephone wire. It was a happy noise and Poppy couldn't stand it. She reached for her wand and turned them all into stone, followed in quick succession by two more cats, a squirrel, and a colony of ants marching across the pavement. The postman was just walking past on the other side of the street, whistling away, and Poppy was about to turn him into stone when a goose waddled out from the path that led down to the canal. Pausing a moment, Poppy suddenly had an idea. She would live in that old abandoned cottage, the one beside the canal with the falling-in roof and broken windows. After all, it didn't belong to anyone and she'd be quite alone there, nobody to bother her. With a determined flick of her wrist, Poppy zapped the poor goose to stone and kicked him under a patch of ferns. Then she marched on by.

As she climbed over the crumbling wall in front of the cottage, Poppy remembered how she and Charlie had sat there talking. They had laughed and eaten cookies, and she had told Charlie about her dreams of one day owning a little bakery just like Patisserie Marie Claire. Not wanting the sadness to overwhelm her, Poppy used the full force of her anger to turn a beautiful swan, floating down the canal, into stone. Then she shoved open the front door and went inside. It was musty and dark. The floorboards had caved in and nettles were growing up between them. There was no furniture in the room except for two old packing crates and a stained, lumpy mattress. Empty cans littered the floor, but someone had swept up all the broken glass into a corner. Obviously Poppy was not the first person to claim the cottage as her home, although from the dust, it seemed whoever had been living here was long gone. The only other occupants now were a family of mice who had chewed a nest for themselves in the middle of the mattress, and Poppy promptly fossilized them.

It was impossible to go upstairs, because most of the boards had rotted away, so Poppy moved one of the packing crates over to a window and sat down. She opened a can of Super Savers meat stew from her backpack and ate it cold. Even though it tasted like dog food, Poppy didn't care. Then, holding her wand at the ready, she turned every bird that landed in the overgrown garden to stone. When it got too dark to see by, she lay down on the damp, lumpy mattress and fell asleep.

A dawn chorus of chirping robins woke Poppy, and within seconds they had joined the rest of the little stone birds outside. Sitting back down on her packing crate, she ate two Twirlies and stared out at the canal. Poppy stayed there all day. By the time the light was fading, she had turned three swans, seventeen ducks, a woodpecker, and a rabbit to stone. Each time she cast the Stop It Now Spell, her sadness faded away a little bit more. In its place was cold, heavy emptiness that stopped her from thinking or feeling. She didn't care anymore, and when she tried to cry, she realized that her own tears had turned to stone and they wouldn't fall.

When she got hungry, Poppy ate a Twirlie bar or

something cold from a can. She made her supplies last for five more days, but the time was coming when she knew she'd have to leave the cottage and find more food. One night, under cover of darkness, Poppy got on her broomstick, grabbed her backpack, and flew to the twenty-four-hour Super Savers Market. She swooped through the front door and headed down the first aisle, filling her backpack with the first cans she came to. Then flying down the next aisle, Poppy reached for some packets of Twirlies and Fudge Monkeys. The cashiers and the manager stared in openmouthed disbelief as she sped past them all without paying.

"Hey, come back here," the manager yelled, starting to chase after the broomstick. He didn't get very far, because Poppy turned him to stone before whizzing through the automatic doors.

When she got back to the cottage, Poppy emptied out her loot onto the floor. There were ten cans of Super Savers stew, twelve boxes of Twirlies, and sixteen packets of Fudge Monkeys.

And so Poppy spent her days, sitting by the window, looking out over the canal. She rarely washed or brushed her hair. Sometimes, in the middle of the night, Poppy would jump into the canal for a quick swim. As soon as they heard her splashing about, the fishes hid among the reeds; otherwise, they knew what would happen to them. The bottom of the canal was already dotted with stone trout and pickerel. Occasionally, on a day when the sun was shining and a warm breeze blew through the window, Poppy would think about Charlie, but she quickly squashed these thoughts by turning a squirrel or a robin into stone. Friends didn't matter now. Nothing mattered. Her old life as Poppy Pendle was over.

Chapter Seventeen

....

Charlie and the Goose

CHARLIE COULDN'T STOP THINKING ABOUT POPPY, no matter how hard she tried. It had been a shock to discover that Poppy had disappeared again. After hanging around Ruthersfield without catching sight of her friend, Charlie came to the sad conclusion that Poppy had once more run away. Only this time she wasn't at Marie Claire's. Charlie had stopped by the patisserie after school one day to see if Poppy was there, and when Marie Claire heard the distressing news, she was beside herself with worry.

"I cannot believe that Poppy has run off again. I should never have let her go," Marie Claire said.

"What else could you do?" Charlie said, trying to make Marie Claire feel better. "Her parents would probably have called the police."

"I don't know, *chérie*." Marie Claire shrugged. "All I know is that after Poppy left, everything seems to have gone wrong. My breads don't rise like they used to and my cakes and pastries taste flat." Marie Claire wiped at a smudge on the counter. "Can you believe my landlord came by on Wednesday to tell me he would not be renewing my lease?" She looked at Charlie out of sad eyes. "It is as if the life has gone out of my bakery, and I blame myself. I really do. It's all my fault. Poppy is meant to be here. She has baking in her blood. I knew that, Charlie, and I let them take her away."

Walking slowly home from Marie Claire's, Charlie wondered for the hundredth time what could possibly have happened to her friend. She had been by the Pendles' house once already. The car was in the driveway, so obviously the Pendles hadn't gone anywhere. She had even glimpsed Mr. and Mrs. Pendle through the kitchen window, but Charlie didn't have the courage to go up and knock on the door. It was all so strange. As she walked past the pathway that led down to the canal, Charlie found herself wishing for a sign. Something that would help her find Poppy. She had been so lonely without her friend. And that's when she came across the goose, its long, curved neck sticking out of a patch of ferns. Charlie crouched down and gently stroked the goose's head. It had a rather surprised look on its stone face, which made Charlie smile. She tugged at the goose, but it was heavy. Too heavy for her to move, so she ran most of the way home and made her father return with his pickup truck. Charlie's dad hauled the stone goose into the back and slowly drove it home.

"Where on earth did you find that?" Charlie's mum asked as they lugged the goose into the back garden.

"Down by the canal path," Charlie said. "Under some bushes, all covered in dirt. Look at his face. Isn't he sweet? I've always wanted a goose for a pet."

"I wonder who would throw such a thing away?" Mrs. Monroe mused, watching her daughter wipe the bird gently down with a damp towel. "Those sorts of garden ornaments are expensive."

"It's beautifully carved," Charlie's dad remarked, running a hand along the goose's back. "Solid stone. Whoever made this was a true craftsman."

"I can keep it, can't I?" Charlie asked, and her parents exchanged a brief look. Both of them nodded. They were happy to see Charlie smiling again. She had been so miserable the past few days, and when her mother asked what the matter was, Charlie had just mumbled, "Friend trouble."

Charlie spent all her free time with the goose. After school she would run straight home to see him. She liked to brush the leaves and dirt off his back and then sit down beside him to eat her snack. Charlie's mum could see her chatting away to the stone bird as if they were having a conversation; which in actual fact they were. Although the goose couldn't talk back, he was an excellent listener, and Charlie felt as if he could somehow understand her.

One afternoon it was raining hard and Charlie dashed out to cover the goose with an umbrella. The next day the temperature dropped and she wrapped him snuggly in a blanket.

"Should we be worried?" Mr. Monroe asked his wife, peering through the kitchen window at their daughter. "That goose seems to be her only friend." He watched in concern as Charlie left half her oatmeal cookie on the ground in front of the stone goose. "She appears to be feeding him," he remarked to his wife as Charlie skipped through the back door.

"I thought he might like something to eat," she said. "Doesn't he look hungry to you?"

"It's a statue, sweetheart," her father replied gently,

but the next morning when Charlie came down for breakfast, the cookie was nowhere in sight. "He ate it!" Charlie shrieked, jumping up and down. "I knew he was hungry. He ate it and he took a little walk."

"Did you move him?" Charlie's mum asked her husband in a whisper, but Mr. Monroe shook his head and gave a puzzled shrug.

That night Charlie fed the goose again. This time she left him out a slice of her mother's fruitcake, and in the morning the cake was gone and the goose had waddled across the grass and was standing under their apple tree. The ground was damp and there were webbed feet marks left in the wet earth. "I think he likes being sheltered from the wind," Charlie said at the breakfast table. "He has a smile on his face now, Mum."

"Well, I'm glad he enjoyed his fruitcake," Mrs. Monroe murmured, not knowing quite what to make of it all.

"Hey, listen to this," Charlie's dad said, reading from the front page of the *Potts Bottom Gazette*. "'A number of lifelike stone animals and birds have been cropping up all over town. No one knows quite where these creatures have come from, but there is talk of witchcraft being involved. It has been reported that a Mr. Darren Smegs, manager of the local Super Savers Market, was turned into stone last Wednesday evening, following a confrontation with a young girl on a broomstick. One of the cashiers has confirmed that the witch in question was wearing a Ruthersfield uniform. Mr. Smegs's wife says she will use her husband as a garden ornament until he recovers. She was quoted as telling the *Gazette* that Mr. Smegs actually makes an impressive stone scarecrow and she's seriously thinking of keeping him that way. A search for the young girl is in progress, and certain staff members at Ruthersfield Academy are helping police with their inquiries. It should also be noted that Police Constable Flower of the Potts Bottom Constabulary seems to have mysteriously disappeared. He was working on this case and was last seen sitting at his desk, eating a ham sandwich for lunch. Further investigations are underway. The *Gazette* has been informed that police are not releasing all information pertaining to this crime at the present moment, due to reasons of security.'"

"I'm late for school," Charlie said, picking up her toast and racing for the door.

"You've half an hour before the bus comes," Mrs. Monroe called after her, but Charlie didn't hear. She was already running down the street and heading straight across town for the Pendles' house.

Chapter Eighteen

....

Garden of Stone

POPPY HAD TO BE THE GIRL ON THE BROOMSTICK. Charlie felt sure of this. She also felt sure that her friend was in trouble. Gathering up her courage, Charlie marched down the Pendles' garden path and knocked on their front door. There was no answer and Charlie knocked again. She could see Mr. and Mrs. Pendle standing in the kitchen just like last time. They weren't moving at all, almost as if they didn't want to be noticed. Charlie had a suspicion they knew she was outside, and had deliberately decided not to answer the door.

"You'll not have much luck," a woman said, leaning

over the garden fence and looking inquisitively at Charlie. "I heard you knocking."

"They won't answer," Charlie said in frustration.

"No."

"But I can see them in the kitchen."

"Are you a friend of Poppy's?"

"Yes." Charlie nodded. "Is she home, do you know?"

The woman studied Charlie for a moment, her lips pursed in disapproval. Then she said in a short, clipped voice, "I'm Maxine from next door. Stay there. I'll be right over." Charlie waited as Maxine trotted down her garden path and straight up the Pendles'.

"There's something you should see," she said, taking a key out of her apron pocket and opening the front door. "Follow me," she instructed, eagerly leading Charlie down the hallway. Looking through to the kitchen, Charlie could see a gaping hole between two cupboards where the oven must have stood, and she felt a fresh burst of anger toward Poppy's parents for doing something so mean. "Don't touch," Maxine ordered, escorting Charlie into the room. Whatever Charlie was about to discover, she had a strong suspicion that Maxine had shown it to plenty of others before her. "There!" Maxine announced dramatically, waving a hand at Mr. and Mrs. Pendle, who were still standing exactly where Poppy had left them.

"Oh!" Charlie exclaimed, covering her mouth in shock. "Oh," she gasped again, feeling slightly sick. "Are they real?" Charlie said, giving a spontaneous shiver. This was not what she had been expecting.

"Depends what you mean by real, doesn't it?" Maxine sniffed, wiping her nose on the edge of her apron. It was cold in the kitchen and the air smelled stale. "So you don't know anything about this, then?"

"No, no, I had no idea." Charlie shook her head in disbelief, holding on to the edge of the table for support.

"Poppy did that to them," Maxine said frostily, although she couldn't hide the ghoulish excitement in her eyes. "Turned her own parents to stone."

"Are you sure it was Poppy?" Charlie questioned, knowing the answer but not quite believing it.

"Course I'm sure. You should have heard the yelling." Maxine shuddered. "Even with my telly on, I could hear them going at it. Who knows what that girl was doing to make her mother so mad. Poppy was a handful all right. Bad influences leading her astray, Edith always reckoned"—and she gave Charlie a hard stare. "Anyway, I'm not surprised she went off the deep end. Poppy was always different, but to turn on your own parents like that. Sooner or later I imagine they'll come out of it. . . ." Maxine's voice trailed off and she shook her head slowly.

Charlie let go of the table and hesitated a moment before cautiously walking up to Mrs. Pendle.

"It's the same stone as my goose," she whispered, reaching out a hand and touching a cold, hard sleeve.

"What did you say?" Maxine pressed nosily. "I can't hear you, and I said not to touch."

"Nothing," Charlie murmured, staring up at Mrs. Pendle's distraught-looking face, which appeared to have been frozen in midchew.

"It's Edith's poor sister, Viv, I feel sorry for," Maxine went on with relish. "She was the one to find them. Fainted dead away and hasn't left her house since." Maxine pulled her cardigan around her and lowered her voice as if someone was listening in. "I think she's worried Poppy will get her next."

Suddenly the kitchen felt stifling. "I have to go," Charlie gasped, stumbling into the hallway. She had to have fresh air.

"Sure you don't know anything about this?" Maxine questioned suspiciously, following after her.

"I'm sorry, I don't, but I hope they're okay," Charlie said, glancing back at the Pendles.

"Well, if you find that friend of yours, you tell her she's wanted by the police. You just can't go around casting spells on innocent people," Maxine said. "It's a criminal offense that is, turning people, and especially your parents, to stone. She'll be sent away to Scrubs when they find her. That's what the police told me."

"So you've spoken to them, have you?" Charlie said, feeling more and more anxious.

"Of course I have." Maxine nodded eagerly. "Went right down to the police station with poor Viv after she'd discovered what Poppy had done. The police aren't talking to the press about it yet, though," Maxine said, sounding slightly disappointed. "Poppy being a minor, and all that. Viv and I have been sworn to secrecy. But they're looking for that girl," she continued. Lowering her voice, Maxine added, "Officer Kibble doesn't want to scare the public either, you see. It might start a mass panic if people thought they were in danger from a crazed witch breaking into their homes."

Charlie suspected that most of Potts Bottom probably knew all about Mr. and Mrs. Pendle already. She had a strong suspicion that Maxine wasn't the best at keeping secrets.

Even though it was a school day, Charlie knew she couldn't face lessons this morning. The shock of what she had just seen was starting to sink in, and she wondered what on earth must have happened to make Poppy turn her parents to stone like that. Something really dreadful, Charlie suspected, folding her arms across her stomach and feeling more and more worried as she walked. Charlie had already missed the school bus, and the thought of turning up late was just unbearable. All the girls would laugh at her. She'd never be able to concentrate, and to make matters worse, she'd forgotten her lunch. As Charlie passed the grassy track that led down toward the canal, she didn't even hesitate before hurrying along it. Nobody went near the canal. She could easily spend the day here without being discovered.

As Charlie walked alongside the water, she remembered the afternoon Poppy had used her magic to make the fish dance. How they had both sat on the little stone wall in front of the tumbledown cottage, and how Poppy had shared her dreams of one day owning a bakery when she grew up. It had been lovely, and Charlie smiled, thinking about the almond crunch bars they had shared. She clambered up onto that same wall now and closed her eyes, swallowing an imaginary taste of crunch bar. A soft sigh escaped through Charlie's lips, and she hoped that wherever Poppy happened to be at this moment, she was happy.

Somewhere close by a car engine backfired, and Charlie spun around, startled by the sudden noise. She gasped and almost fell off the wall, but not because of the explosion. Scattered across the overgrown lawn behind her were hundreds of stone animals and birds. Just like her goose. There were blackbirds and blue tits, sparrows and robins. One of the robins even had a tiny stone worm in its mouth. Charlie couldn't quite believe what she was seeing. A stone cat stood ready to pounce in the long grass, and numerous stone squirrels clung to the branches of the surrounding trees. Most shocking of all was a whole flock of stone ducks at the end of the garden, their wings still spread out as if they had only just landed. Too stunned to move, Charlie sat on the wall and stared. She stared and stared, until she realized she was holding her breath. Then, taking in a great lungful of air, she wondered what on earth she should do. Could Poppy be behind this? Perhaps she had used the cottage to hide in. Maybe she was there right now, baking up something delicious to eat.

"Poppy," Charlie called, breaking the silence. There was no answer, so Charlie lowered herself down onto the other side of the wall. She almost stepped on a stone rabbit and let out a nervous cry of distress. All these stone animals made her think of a graveyard. If it hadn't been sunny and early in the morning, Charlie would certainly have bolted.

She picked her way over to the cottage, trying to avoid the patches of nettles and broken glass. It wasn't easy, and Charlie bit back a yelp as she stung herself on a particularly fierce plant. Suddenly the idea of anyone living here seemed ridiculous. There couldn't be any heat or running water in the cottage, let alone an oven. This place was a dump, but nonetheless Charlie skirted a sprawling holly bush, thinking she'd have a quick peek through one of the windows. And that's when she stumbled right into the crouched hidden figure of a stone policeman. She covered her mouth in horror, letting out a soft moan. PC Flower, his stone name tag read, and Charlie knew at once that she had found the missing police officer. He had a truncheon clutched in one hand and a look of stunned surprise on his face. For a few moments Charlie stood perfectly still, feeling too horrified to move. PC Flower was staring straight up at the window, and suddenly Charlie didn't want to know what he had been looking at. But she had to know. She had to find out. Holding her breath in along with her rising panic, Charlie tiptoed past the policeman. Then before she lost her nerve, she grabbed on to the stone window ledge and pulled herself up.

Peering through the open window, Charlie screamed and let go, dropping back down sharply, and grazing her arm on the wall. What she had seen was more disturbing than the garden full of stone animals, even more disturbing than PC Flower. A girl her age sat hunched by the window on a packing crate. One of her hands grasped a magic wand, the other a half-eaten Fudge Monkey. Empty cans and Twirlie bar wrappers littered the floor around her, and there was a nasty smell of stew in the air.

Bravely pulling herself up for another look, Charlie ignored the pain in her arm. There was no sound from inside, and the girl didn't move. For a moment Charlie wondered if she, too, was made out of stone. Then slowly, very slowly, the girl raised her head. She stared up at Charlie out of vacant, empty eyes, and Charlie realized with a start that it was Poppy!

"Poppy, it's me," Charlie panted, holding on tight to the window ledge. Her arms were aching, and her stomach was starting to hurt from pressing against the rough stone. "I've been so worried about you." Still, the eyes looking up at her didn't register any emotion. The girl looked like Poppy but her eyes were someone else's. They were as blank as a piece of untouched paper. "Poppy, it's me," Charlie repeated in a louder voice, beginning to feel scared. "I want to help you, please." She wished her friend would say something, anything, even if it was to tell her to go away. But Poppy kept on staring at Charlie as if she were invisible.

"Look at me," Charlie shouted. "I'm right here, Poppy. Look at me."

Then without warning, Poppy suddenly blinked and raised her wand in the air, croaking out, "Consticrabi-haltus." Letting go, Charlie dropped abruptly onto the grass again, squealing as a gray thunderbolt whizzed by her ear. She whipped around to see it hit a starling that had landed in the tree behind her. Almost immediately the starling froze and faded to the color of bleak stone, its beak hanging open as if it was about to sing. Not waiting to see any more, Charlie turned and ran.

She had never been a particularly fast runner, but if her gym teacher were watching now, he would certainly have signed her up for the track team. Charlie ran and ran, expecting to be turned into stone at any second. Her legs ached and her stomach cramped, but still she ran on. Straight through the center of Potts Bottom and past Patisserie Marie Claire, Charlie sprinted.

Nosy old Maxine had said she was to go to the police if she found Poppy. Well, Charlie had no intention of doing any such thing. This wasn't a police matter, as far as she was concerned. It was a case of magic gone too far. What she needed to do now was find out what sort of magic Poppy was using. Then maybe she could help her friend to stop.

Chapter Nineteen

A Dangerous Witch

CHARLIE CLATTERED UP THE WIDE GRANITE STEPS OF Ruthersfield Academy, and pushed against the door. It was locked. She pulled on the bell rope before she could change her mind. The clang, clang, clang of a somber bell rang out from inside. Footsteps could be heard, and Charlie stood gasping for breath as she waited for someone to come.

A girl dressed in the purple and gold school uniform opened the heavy door. "Yes?" She looked down at Charlie with a condescending sneer.

"I'd like to talk to the headmistress, please."

"Excuse me?" The girl gave a superior snort of

laughter. "You're not a Ruthersfield girl, are you." This was a statement, not a question, and Charlie's confidence immediately started to crumble. Then she remembered Poppy, with her dirty, matted hair and half-eaten Fudge Monkey. Who else was there to help her friend?

"No, no, I'm not, but I still need to speak with the headmistress."

"And what is this about?" the girl asked, examining her long purple nails.

"It's p-p-p-private," Charlie stammered.

"Because you're obviously not magic, are you, and you can't attend Ruthersfield unless you've got the gift."

"I don't want to come here," Charlie explained, noticing a woman in a long flowing cloak walking with clipped, purposeful strides across the hallway behind the girl. She looked official, like a teacher, and raising her voice so the woman could hear, Charlie said loudly, "I need to talk to someone. It's about Poppy Pendle."

"Poppy Pendle," the woman broke in, hurrying over and brushing aside the girl with the purple nails. "Shouldn't you be in history class, Deirdre?"

"Yes, Miss Weedle, but I heard the bell ring and nobody else was around."

"Well, you can go now, Deirdre, thank you. I'll

handle this." Bending down so her face was level with Charlie's, she said, "You have information on Poppy Pendle?"

"Yes," Charlie whispered, feeling nervous.

"Come with me, please," the woman said briskly, motioning for Charlie to follow her. "This is a matter for Ms. Roach."

As they hurried past the girl called Deirdre, she narrowed her eyes at Charlie, flipped back her long dark hair and gave another spectacular sneer. Or maybe that was just how her face always looked. *No wonder Poppy hates it here,* Charlie thought. Worst of all, there didn't seem to be any windows to let light in, so it was as dark and stuffy as a cardboard box.

"Here we are," Miss Weedle, the spells and charms teacher, announced, coming to a halt in front of a padded green leather door. She knocked once and immediately pushed down the brass handle, ushering Charlie inside. "Emergency," she mouthed to the woman sitting behind a desk. "We need to speak to Ms. Roach right now."

"She's on a conference call," the desk person said, flipping shut a magazine and shuffling some papers about in a flustered manner. "I can't disturb her."

"Well, I can," Miss Weedle pronounced, marching straight past the desk and opening the door beyond it.

A tall, thin woman with small round glasses was holding a phone up to her ear and frowning. Her frown got deeper and she glared at the intruders, waving them away with a flick of her wrist. She covered the mouthpiece and hissed, "Busy!"

"It's about Poppy," Miss Weedle said, rolling her eyes in Charlie's direction.

"I'll call you back," the headmistress snapped, abruptly hanging up the telephone. "Newspaper reporters," she grumbled. "All the daily press are hounding me for interviews. They know a Ruthersfield girl is involved, of course. I'm trying to keep this thing contained, but an evil witch is big news. Especially one who has turned to the dark side at such a young age." Adjusting her glasses, she studied Charlie through them. "Would someone please care to explain what is going on here?"

"Well, go on," Miss Weedle prompted, pacing nervously about the room. "Sit down and tell us what you know." Charlie collapsed into one of the chairs opposite Ms. Roach.

"I just want to help Poppy," she said, feeling tears well up in her eyes. "Only I don't know how."

"But you know where she is?" Ms. Roach questioned, leaning over the desk. "Because it's important you tell us."

"I d-d-d-don't want to get Poppy into trouble," Charlie stammered. "I'm just scared because she seemed so, so . . ." She stopped and thought hard for a moment, trying to come up with the right word. "She seemed so lost."

"Lost!" Ms. Roach and Miss Weedle said at the same time.

"Yes, her hair was a mess, and I don't think she'd changed her clothes in quite a while. She didn't seem to recognize me, and," Charlie added with emphasis, "she was eating a Fudge Monkey." Neither Ms. Roach nor Miss Weedle seemed to understand the full significance of this.

Ms. Roach finally murmured, "Well, go on."

"I believe she's turned her parents to stone," Charlie whispered, wondering how much she should tell them. "She seems to have turned a lot of things to stone."

"We know," Ms. Roach sighed, "and it's becoming a bit of a problem. I've already had the police round here asking questions. Did you hear about the manager at the local Super Savers Market?"

"My dad read about him in the newspaper this morning."

"Then you understand that this does not look good for Ruthersfield," Ms. Roach continued. "We are a school with a superb reputation in witchcraft," she said, speaking as if she had lockjaw. Her face was so tense Charlie could see a big blue vein throbbing at the side of her neck. "Most of our girls go on to have brilliant careers in magic, and we have many Noblet Prize winners among our alumnae." She shook her head sadly. "In fact, Poppy Pendle was destined for great things."

"But she doesn't like magic," Charlie pointed out. "She doesn't want to be a witch."

"Oh, that's nonsense," Ms. Roach said. "Utter nonsense. Poppy was one of our finest witches."

"But she doesn't enjoy it," Charlie stressed. "Magic makes her miserable. She wants to be a baker, only her parents won't let her. She's furious with them. That's why she ran away. She never had tonsillitis at all."

"She ran away!" Ms. Roach looked shocked. "I must admit I thought it was odd when her mother told us Poppy had been sick, because she's never missed a day of school before. We had no idea she ran away. Of course there was talk amongst the girls," Ms. Roach admitted. "But we didn't believe such rumors for a moment. Her parents never said a word."

"Well, that explains a lot," Miss Weedle said, sinking down onto a chair beside Charlie. "It certainly explains why the Stop It Now Spell worked so well with her. All that pent-up fury and aggression." She shuddered. "I thought she was just having a bad day. I would never have taught it if I'd realized quite how unhappy she was."

"Is that the spell that turns things into stone?" Charlie asked, and Miss Weedle looked vaguely embarrassed.

"It's basically a safety spell," she said defensively. "We use it to halt things that are out of control. Most of our girls have a hard enough time actually getting an object to stop. It's not an easy one to master," she told them. "And you usually need years of experience to transform things into stone. Even I can't do that."

"Except Poppy seemed to manage it without any trouble at all," Ms. Roach said in a rather acid tone. "Which is why we find ourselves in this unfortunate situation."

"So how can we help her?" Charlie asked again. "There must be a way to stop her doing what she's doing?"

"Not really," Miss Weedle sighed. "There's no reversal charm for this type of spell."

"I don't understand what you mean." Charlie said.

Miss Weedle slipped a ring on and off her finger. "It's complicated," she said. "There is of course an antidote to the basic Stop It Now Spell. You can freeze something, and then unfreeze it again, a moving car, a mouse, a rolling ball. But once the object has been turned into stone, the antidote won't work, I'm afraid. Too much emotion behind the spell."

"So what about her parents?" Charlie questioned. "What about the manager of Super Savers and all those animals and birds?"

"Only Poppy has the power to change those things back."

"How?" Charlie cried. "How can she do that if there's no reversal charm, or whatever you call it?"

"It's not going to be easy," Miss Weedle admitted. "The spell is a deep one. This sort of magic is extremely powerful, and more so when it's used for an evil cause."

"Turning her parents to stone wasn't evil," Charlie interrupted hotly. "They were awful to Poppy. They deserved it."

"That may be true," Miss Weedle acknowledged, "but the answer is still the same. This particular spell can only be undone by Poppy." Here she stopped and gave a troubled sigh. "And to do that she needs to identify where the force behind the spell came from and reverse it. Undo that energy."

"We know where it came from," Charlie said. "She was working at Patisserie Marie Claire and her parents dragged her back home. She didn't want to leave." Charlie scowled at Ms. Roach as if she was partly responsible. "Poppy was really upset. That's all she's ever wanted to do, bake, and now she'll never cook again."

"So to reverse the Stop It Now Spell," Miss Weedle said somberly, "Poppy needs to get rid of her anger, that particular anger. The one that's driving her fury."

"That's the problem." Charlie's voice shook. "That's why I came here. I don't think Poppy wants to stop doing what she's doing. I think she's given up. I mean, she's eating Fudge Monkeys and Twirlies."

"Well then, we have a serious crisis," Miss Weedle said gravely. "Once witches go over to the dark side, it is almost impossible to help them get back again, unless they are willing to change. Most of them, I'm afraid, are not."

Reaching for Charlie's hand, Ms. Roach gave it a gentle squeeze. "You must tell us where Poppy is, before she hurts anyone else. The police want her locked behind bars, and I must say I'm inclined to agree with them. Although," she added wistfully, "it is a tragic waste of a beautiful mind. Right from the beginning I knew that girl had special talent."

"Yes, she does," Charlie agreed. "She makes the most delicious cakes and cookies in the world. That's what her talent is and that's what she loves." She looked imploringly over at the headmistress. "Please, Ms. Roach, don't call the police yet. Now that I understand about the spell Poppy's using, I honestly think I can help her. Please let me try. I'm sure if Poppy starts baking again, she'll be happy. That's all she wants. That's why she's so upset," Charlie said, standing up and twisting a frizzy curl round her finger. "Once Poppy begins to cook, she won't be angry anymore and the spell will reverse itself, and everything will be fine. She always said it was impossible to make a good cake if you're in a bad mood."

"Did she now?" Ms. Roach muttered, leaning back in her chair and rubbing her eyes. "Very well, child, I will grant you a few more days, but only because I would like to contain this scandal. If anyone else gets turned to stone in the meantime"—she leveled her gaze at Charlie—"we call in the police and you tell them where Poppy is."

"Okay." Charlie nodded, shaking Ms. Roach's hand and trying not to think about PC Flower.

Then, hurrying out of Ruthersfield Academy, Charlie sprinted straight for Marie Claire's.

Chapter Twenty

· ·

An Idea

THERE WERE LIGHTS ON IN THE SHOP, BUT CHARLIE couldn't see any people. Usually at this time in the morning, Patisserie Marie Claire was jammed with customers. *"Bonjour,"* Marie Claire said, glancing up from behind the counter. "Ah, Charlie, hello. Should you not be in school?"

"I've found Poppy," Charlie panted. "Down by the canal in that empty cottage. She's all by herself and her clothes are all dirty. She's been eating Fudge Monkeys."

Marie Claire gasped. "Fudge Monkeys, Charlie. This is serious."

"It's worse than that. She's the one who's been going around turning all the animals and birds in Potts Bottom to stone." Charlie paused for breath. "She turned her parents to stone and a manager at the Super Savers Market. And you know that police officer who disappeared?" Charlie said.

"I read about him this morning," Marie Claire murmured.

"Well, he's hidden behind a bush by the cottage. She's turned him to stone as well. Which means it probably won't be long before the rest of the police force discovers her."

"Mon Dieu!" Marie Claire walked over to the door and flipped the closed sign around. "Now we can talk without being disturbed."

"But what about your customers?" Charlie said in concern.

"What customers?" Marie Claire looked around the shop. "Since Poppy left, my baking has not been the same."

"That's because you miss her," Charlie pointed out.

"Perhaps," Marie Claire agreed. "Certainly my heart isn't in it. Did you not read the sign out front?" She gestured at the window. "I have to close next month. My landlord won't renew the lease. He wants to put a MockTurdles Burger Palace in here."

"That's horrible." Charlie grimaced. "Poppy would be so upset if she knew."

"Have you talked with her?" Marie Claire asked. "Would she accept a visit from me, do you think?"

"She won't talk at all," Charlie said. "That's the problem. She's so unhappy, Marie Claire. This spell Poppy's been putting on everything is incredibly powerful. I think it's taken her over in some way, and there doesn't seem to be anything anyone can do about it." Charlie helped herself to a chocolate croissant from the display case and took a bite. It was dry and rather bland. Not like the croissants Marie Claire used to make.

"How do you know this, Charlie?" Marie Claire said.

"Because I've just been to Ruthersfield. I thought they might have a way to help. At least to change back all the animals and birds Poppy turned to stone. Not that I care about those parents of hers," Charlie muttered. "If it were up to me, I'd keep them stone forever."

"And what did they tell you, Charlie? There must be something we can do to help her."

"She's gone over to the dark side," Charlie said soberly, "and it's almost impossible to get her back, according to Ms. Roach, the headmistress. All the things she's turned to stone will have to stay that way."

"Forever?" Marie Claire looked flabbergasted.

"Unless Poppy can take the energy she used to create that spell in the first place and turn it around. Make it positive."

"And how is she supposed to do that when she won't talk and she's eating Fudge Monkeys?" Marie Claire asked.

"Well, I think we might be able to help her," Charlie said. "Right now Poppy is miserable because her parents dragged her away from here. They took the oven out of their house."

"Ohhh-la-la!" Marie Claire shook her head.

"That's where Poppy's anger has come from," Charlie continued. "And it's why she's turning things to stone."

"So what can we do?"

"Okay, this is my idea," Charlie told her, perching on a stool behind the counter. "We have to make Poppy want to cook again. She's lost all her passion, and that's the problem. If she starts to care, to want to bake cookies and cakes like before, then her anger will disappear and the stone spell should reverse itself. Poppy will be happy, and, and . . ." Charlie shrugged.

"And we'll all live happily ever after?" Marie Claire finished for her, but she was only half teasing, and she reached down to give Charlie a hug.

"I don't know about that," Charlie said sheepishly.

"But we have to try, Marie Claire. If we don't help Poppy, no one else will, and she'll end up in prison."

"*D'accord*! All right!" Marie Claire clapped her hands in a show of efficiency. "Let's head to the kitchen and make her something extra delicious. The way to melt Poppy's anger is clearly through her stomach, and that won't be easy if she's eating Fudge Monkeys."

"And Twirlies," Charlie added with a shudder. "There were Twirlie wrappers everywhere."

They spent the rest of the morning making rich buttery brioche dough filled with chunks of dark chocolate. When the loaves came out of the oven, Marie Claire smiled. She broke one in half to let the steam out and put a hot chunk in her mouth. "Oh my, that's good," she groaned, taking another bite. "I seem to have my touch back again!"

Taking down an old wicker basket from one of the shelves, Marie Claire packed the brioche loaves inside, covered them with a clean cloth, and handed the basket to Charlie. "Would you like me to come with you, *chérie*?"

"I think I should go alone," Charlie said. "We don't want to overwhelm her."

"Well, come back and tell me what happens. This brioche is bound to make Poppy smile when she tastes it."

Filled with a sense of hope, Charlie walked down to

the canal and climbed over the stone wall. There was a rusty iron gate leading up to the cottage, but thick clumps of nettles grew around it, so going through the gate was not a smart idea. Just as before, no sound came from the cottage, but Charlie did see a new addition to Poppy's stone collection. Standing in the overgrown yard was a beautiful stone fox, holding his bushy stone tail aloft. "Poor old thing," Charlie whispered, stroking the fox's head. Carefully picking her way over to the window, Charlie edged around the holly bush, averting her gaze from PC Flower. At least he was well hidden. She stretched up and balanced the basket on the ledge. It wobbled a little, being rather too wide for the narrow sill. She could glimpse Poppy, still sitting on the packing crate. Only this time she had her back to the window and was slurping stew right from a can. As Charlie turned away, she heard a soft thud, and when she looked round, she realized that the basket had tipped over, falling inside the cottage. Then there was a scraping sound as if the packing crate had been kicked across the floor. This was followed by handfuls of brioche flying out of the window as Poppy chucked them into the yard. "Consticrabihaltus," a gruff voice screamed, and the pastries were chased through the air by the Stop It Now Spell. Gray, sparking thunderbolts blazed across the sky. Cowering in the grass, Charlie covered her head with her hands while heavy stone brioche rained down around her.

"Not very successful," Marie Claire sighed when Charlie reported back what had happened.

"I think it scared her when the basket tipped over, but I've had another idea," Charlie said. "Let's make some cakes that look like Twirlies but taste delicious. We'll fool her into eating them because they're Twirlies, but one mouthful and she'll remember how good food can be."

"Mmmmmm." Marie Claire mulled over the suggestion. "It won't be easy because she doesn't want to remember, Charlie. That would hurt too much and bring back all her lost dreams. So our Twirlies will have to be spectacular if we are going to make her feel happiness again."

Marie Claire made a golden sponge cake batter, piped it into log shapes, baked them, and filled the little cakes with sweet vanilla cream. They looked remarkably similar to Twirlie bars. "Leave them outside the door this time," Marie Claire advised. "Poppy will be bound to find them. I must say I'm rather proud of these," she said, taking a bite of cake. "If anything will bring Poppy back from the dark side, a taste of my Twirlie bars should."

* * * *

Charlie carefully positioned a plastic shopping bag full of Marie Claire's Twirlie bars right outside the cottage door. By this time the light had begun to fade, and she knew she would have to get home before her mother began to worry. There was no sign of Poppy, and Charlie didn't want to look through the window again. So instead she knocked on the door and quickly ran away, planning to return the following morning to check if the Twirlies had been taken.

Chapter Twenty-One

....

An Oven to Cook With

WHEN CHARLIE ARRIVED HOME, HER MOTHER MET HER at the front door, looking worried. "Where were you?" Mrs. Monroe burst out. "Your teacher just called." She gave Charlie a penetrating look. "Apparently, you weren't in school today, which is odd considering how early you left the house."

"I'm sorry," Charlie apologized. "I missed the bus because I had to go and see Poppy. I was worried about her. She's, well, she's been having trouble lately." Charlie found that her eyes had filled with tears. "And I forgot my lunch and I hate walking into class late."

"So you took the whole day off?" Mrs. Monroe said more gently.

"I'm really sorry, Mum. It won't happen again, I promise. I was just trying to help Poppy."

Mrs. Monroe gave her daughter a tight hug. "Is everything all right with her?"

"I don't think so," Charlie said. "Which is why I'm trying to help."

After supper that night Charlie left a piece of buttered soda bread by her goose. In the morning the bread was gone, and he had waddled around to the other side of the apple tree. She didn't understand why he should move about at night, but Marie Claire said it was probably because Charlie and Poppy had been such good friends. "You girls have a special connection," she told Charlie, who had gone straight to Marie Claire's after breakfast. "The goose can sense that. Besides, if it's food and love that will melt away Poppy's anger, and that's what you're giving your goose, well, it makes sense, *n'est-ce pas*? You soften his heart enough so that he can walk a little at night. And let us not forget that those dark hours are a time when magic is at its most powerful."

"Do you think I could make him real again?" Charlie wondered, and Marie Claire shook her head.

"Only Poppy can do that, but perhaps our Twirlies

have worked, *chérie*? Why don't you go and see?"

Thank goodness it was a Saturday, so there was no school for Charlie. With a churning stomach, she headed over to the canal, anxious about what she would find. At the bottom of the grassy track that led down from the road, Charlie stopped. She stood quite still, staring in the direction of the cottage. The door was opening and she watched as Poppy appeared, blinking in the sunlight and shielding her eyes from the early morning glare. It had worked! Charlie was just about to shout something out when she noticed the plastic bag of Twirlies still lying on the grass where she'd left it the night before. So Poppy hadn't seen them yet. Well, she would now, but Poppy paid no attention to the bag at all. She ran down to the canal and jumped in fully clothed, clutching her magic wand. Now Charlie was worried. No one went swimming in the canal. The sides were straight and steep and the water was a dark, murky green. She could see a family of ducks floating down, and Charlie watched in distress as Poppy whipped out her wand and yelled, "Consticrabihaltus." The ducks immediately turned to stone, and Poppy picked them up, throwing them onto the bank. They landed among the reeds with a succession of dull thuds. Then, after dunking her head under the water, she climbed out again, shaking herself vigorously like a dog. Looking neither left nor right, Poppy stormed up the bank. Even her walk was filled with a fury that made Charlie nervous just to watch. With a massive leap, she vaulted over the stone wall and marched straight back to the cottage, ignoring the bag of Twirlies as she stomped inside.

"Oh no!" Charlie groaned softly. Poppy hadn't even tried one. For a brief instant she considered trying to talk to Poppy again, but the thought of that blank face and those dull, unseeing eyes stopped her. There was no point in going back to the cottage just yet, not unless she wanted to be turned into stone. Charlie didn't actually believe that Poppy would use the Stop It Now Spell on her, but she wasn't going to risk it.

Marie Claire sighed with disappointment when she heard what had happened to the Twirlies. "And they were so good too," she said. "I just know Poppy would have loved them."

"So, what next?" Charlie questioned, slumping over Marie Claire's butcher-block worktable. "I'm so worried that Poppy's going to turn someone else into stone, and then it'll be too late. I'll have to tell the police where she is, and poor Poppy will end up in jail."

"No, no, we cannot let that happen," Marie Claire said, pummeling a mound of bread dough. "Last night

I couldn't sleep, and so I did a lot of thinking. Too much thinking," she added, wiping the back of her hand across her forehead and leaving it streaked with flour. Charlie noticed that Marie Claire had dark, bluish circles under her eyes, and her skin looked puffy with tiredness. "I believe that what Poppy needs is an oven," Marie Claire said, shaping the dough into baguettes. "Once she starts baking again, she won't be able to stay angry for long."

"But that's impossible," Charlie said, squishing a piece of dough between her fingers. "There's no electricity in the cottage, and how on earth would we get an oven hooked up?"

"Yes, it won't be easy," Marie Claire agreed. "But it's not impossible, either. I have a small gas oven we can use that runs from its own little canister of propane gas. I cook with it when the electricity goes out so I can still bake my breads." Marie Claire thought for a moment, then continued. "We could deliver it at night when Poppy is sleeping. She may be a witch, but she still needs to sleep. I'll put together a box of baking supplies, the best Normandy butter, some of my special bittersweet chocolate, flour and sugar of course, and some fresh local eggs." Marie Claire sounded excited, and Charlie couldn't help thinking that it just might work.

"Let's give her a cookie sheet and some cake pans," Charlie added, beginning to feel enthusiastic about the plan.

"The only problem," Marie Claire murmured, chewing on her lip, "is how to carry it in. I couldn't lift an oven, and neither could you."

"We could ask my dad," Charlie suggested. "I'm sure he'd help. He has a pickup truck, and he's really strong."

"Mmmm." Marie Claire pondered this for a moment. "He'd have to know about Poppy," she said at last. "We couldn't lie to him about that. It's too dangerous."

"Oh, he won't mind. I know he won't. Not if it means helping my friend."

"Then we shall ask him together," Marie Claire said, taking Charlie's hand and giving it an optimistic pat. "Come on. No time to waste. But you must tell your father everything that has happened."

After listening to the full story from Charlie and Marie Claire, Mr. Monroe sighed and shook his head. "I'm sorry, Charlie. I don't think I can do this. It's a police matter now, by the sound of things."

"Dad, you've always taught me to trust my instincts," Charlie said, "and Poppy is a good, kind girl. I can't abandon her."

"Mr. Monroe," Marie Claire said quietly. "Your daughter is right about Poppy. And everyone deserves a second chance, don't you think?"

"Please?" Charlie pleaded, pressing her hands together hard.

Mr. Monroe looked at his daughter for a long moment. Then he smiled and said, "Very well, Charlie. If your mother agrees, I'll help you move the oven. Poppy Pendle can have her second chance."

Mrs. Monroe took a little more convincing. "I've heard about witches who cross over to the dark side," she worried aloud. "I know Poppy was your friend, honey—"

"Is my friend," Charlie corrected.

"Is your friend, but this makes me nervous. Getting an oven into that cottage without disturbing her will be like trying to step over a sleeping dragon. What if she wakes up and turns you all to stone?"

"Mum, we have to do this," Charlie begged. "It's our only chance. When Poppy sees the little oven and all the wonderful ingredients, she won't be able to stop herself from making cookies. I know her so well, Mum, and once Poppy starts baking, she'll stop being angry. It's the only way we can reverse the spell and get her back."

"Do you really think so?" Mrs. Monroe looked skeptical.

"She's my friend," Charlie stated. "Poppy helped me

the first day I met her. She rescued my sneakers from a tree. That's what friends do. They help each other."

"Well, this is a little more risky than rescuing a pair of sneakers," Charlie's mum pointed out, but she couldn't help thinking it would be nice for her daughter to have a real friend again. As far as she was concerned, Charlie was spending far too much time talking to a stone goose.

So later on that afternoon Charlie's dad drove his truck down to the patisserie. He maneuvered Marie Claire's small white oven and a canister of propane gas onto a handcart and pushed them outside. Then, with the help of Charlie and Marie Claire, he loaded the things into the back of his truck. Charlie had helped Marie Claire assemble an enormous box of baking supplies. There were fat, moist vanilla beans from Madagascar, powdered sugar with which to make frosting, juicy organic lemons, as well as bags of flour and sugar and pots of local cream. Marie Claire had also put in two cookie sheets, three cake pans, a cupcake tin, and mini brioche molds. She even remembered a mixing bowl, wooden spoons, measuring cups, and a wire whisk. "There!" Marie Claire said with a nod of satisfaction. "How can Poppy resist when she sees all these wonderful goodies."

✶ ✶ ✶ ✶

They planned to wait until early the following morning for delivery. Around three a.m., Mr. Monroe decided, when it would still be dark and Poppy should be sleeping. Mrs. Monroe had sent Charlie to bed early that night, insisting she get some rest. "You still need your sleep, Charlie," she had said. "Especially if you plan to go chasing around Potts Bottom later on."

"But I'm not the least bit tired, Mum," Charlie had grumbled as she climbed into bed. She was sure she would never get to sleep, but at some point Charlie did doze off because the next thing she knew her father was gently shaking her awake, whispering for her to get dressed.

Marie Claire stood waiting outside the patisserie for them, wearing a long black cloak and a black wool hat. "I know this will work," Charlie said as they bounced along in the truck. There were no other cars on the road, and it felt strange to be out at such an early hour. As they turned toward the canal, Mr. Monroe cut the truck's engine.

"We can coast down here," he said. "No need to make unnecessary noise." They rolled down the bumpy pathway and came to a stop at the bottom. "Now, you two can wait in the truck."

"No, Dad, I'm coming," Charlie whispered. "You need help."

"I'll be fine, Charlie. You and Marie Claire are to stay in the truck. This isn't a game."

"But how will you get the oven over the wall without Poppy hearing?" Charlie questioned softly. "You can't go through the gate, Dad. It's surrounded by nettles."

"I'll figure it out," Mr. Monroe said, and they all sat in the truck for a moment, staring at the shadowy cottage. It wasn't as dark as they had hoped for. The sky was beautifully clear, lit up by the silvery glow from a full moon.

"What's that?" Charlie suddenly whispered, pointing at a dark shape that had swooped out of the cottage window. "It looks like an enormous bat."

"It's Poppy!" Marie Claire gasped as the silhouette of a girl on a broomstick flew overhead. They could see her long, tangled hair flying out behind her, but she didn't look down or appear to notice the truck. Her hands gripped the broomstick, and the determined set of her jaw was clearly visible in the queer silvery light.

"She looks like she knows where she's going," Charlie's dad said as they watched her disappear in the direction of Potts Bottom.

"I wonder where," Charlie whispered, holding tight to her father's arm.

"No time to worry about that now. Come on, let's shift this oven inside. Who knows how long she'll be gone."

Since Poppy had clearly left the cottage, Marie Claire and Charlie helped out by carrying the supplies. In fact, they all agreed it would probably have been impossible to move the oven into the cottage without Poppy hearing. Charlie's dad had on long, thick work gloves and tall rubber boots. He kicked open the gate and wheeled the oven through on the handcart, plowing down nettles and bumping his way over the tall grass. There were so many stone creatures in the garden it was difficult to find a clear path. So Charlie walked ahead, carefully moving the animals and birds aside. She tried not to think about PC Flower, still crouched out of sight behind the holly bush. When they got to the front door, Charlie felt her legs go weak and a sick feeling lurched in her stomach. Even though they had seen Poppy leave on her broomstick, and she wanted to help her friend, she was still nervous about going in.

It was Marie Claire who opened the door and entered first, followed by Mr. Monroe and the oven, and then Charlie. Luckily, Charlie's dad had remembered to bring a flashlight with him, and he switched it on. *"Mon Dieu!"* Marie Claire murmured as the powerful beam picked up empty cans of stew, Twirlie wrappers, and Fudge Monkey boxes scattered across the floor.

"I did tell you," Charlie whispered.

"Poor thing," Marie Claire sighed. "What are these

Fudge Monkeys?" she asked, picking up an empty box and peering at the ingredients list. "This is not food." Marie Claire sounded horrified as she read the back of the packet. "There is nothing in here but chemicals! Additives! Preservatives!"

"They have a shelf life of forever," Charlie's dad said. "Twirlies never go bad, and, besides, I loved them as a kid," he confessed quietly. "Still do every once in a while."

"Disgusting!" Marie Claire shuddered. "Poppy must be out of her mind. Let us set up the oven at once. This eating of Fudge Monkeys cannot go on."

They cleared out a corner of the room to make space for the stove to stand. Mr. Monroe made sure the gas tank was hooked up, and Charlie carefully arranged all the supplies on one of the empty packing cases. Then they stood back to admire the effect. It looked ridiculously out of place with its white enamel door and shiny chrome burners. "Oh, it's perfect!" Charlie said, skipping about in excitement. She gave her father a hug. "Thank you for helping," she whispered into his shirt.

Mr. Monroe ruffled Charlie's curls. "Let's hope Poppy Pendle makes the most of her second chance, eh!"

"I really think this will work. I really do," Charlie said, and she couldn't stop herself from wondering what Poppy would bake first.

Chapter Twenty-Two

....

A Bag of Almond Cakes

ON THE DRIVE BACK HOME CHARLIE STUCK HER HEAD out the window, staring up at the sky. She was trying to spot Poppy flying around on her broomstick. "I do wonder where she went," Charlie said, but it wasn't until the next morning that the answer became clear. Mr. Monroe almost choked on his toast and marmalade as he read aloud from the front page of the *Potts Bottom Gazette*. "'Early this morning at around three thirty a.m., a robbery took place at the Super Savers Market. Several canned goods and Twirlie bars were taken from the shop. Police did respond to the alarm call, but no one was arrested. Unfortunately, two officers and a stock boy were discovered at the scene of the crime, all of them having been turned to stone. It is thought that this break-in is connected to an incident last Wednesday, when a Mr. Darren Smegs, the manager of Super Savers, was also turned to stone. Police are still searching for a young girl on a broomstick, whom the *Gazette* can now report is believed to be Poppy Pendle of Ten Pudding Lane. Miss Pendle's parents have also been turned to stone, and if anyone has information on the whereabouts of Poppy Pendle, please contact the police station immediately. Constable Flower, who was working on the case, is still reported missing. The endangerment of a police officer is punishable by life imprisonment. At this point, the inquiry has been handed over to higher authorities.'"

"Oh no!" Charlie wailed, pushing aside her Rice Krispies. She had suddenly lost her appetite. "This is awful. I must go and tell Marie Claire at once."

As soon as she opened the patisserie door, Charlie knew Marie Claire had read the headlines. There was no one else in the shop, and poor Marie Claire was hunched over the counter, staring at a copy of the *Potts Bottom Gazette*. When she looked up, her face was drained of color. "We must go down to the canal at once," Marie

Claire said. "I only hope it is not too late and Poppy hasn't been discovered."

Not even bothering to lock the patisserie door, Marie Claire and Charlie hurried through the village. As they started down the canal path Charlie sniffed the air and said hopefully, "I think I can smell cookies."

"We'll know soon enough," Marie Claire muttered, but the answer quickly became obvious. Whatever Charlie had smelled, it certainly wasn't cookies baked in the little gas oven, because blocking the middle of the track was the stove. Only it wasn't shiny white enamel anymore. It was smooth gray stone, and scattered around it were stone bags of sugar, stone eggs, a stone whisk, and even a stone bar of chocolate. Marie Claire and Charlie stared at the carnage in horror. "Oh my, oh my." Marie Claire sank down on the grass. "This is awful, really awful." She buried her face in her hands. Then after a moment she whispered, "How do you think she got it out here?"

"Threw it," Charlie said in a dull voice. "You forget how strong Poppy is. She could lift anything." Sinking down on the grass beside Marie Claire, Charlie began to cry. Not great heaving sobs, but quietly, as if the hope was leaking out of her. "They're going to take Poppy away now, aren't they? Ms. Roach will make me tell the police where she is, and they'll lock her up in Scrubs.

Oh, it's just not fair," Charlie sobbed, beginning to sound angry. "I thought this would work, I really did."

"I did too, *chérie*." Marie Claire sighed. "I did too."

Charlie sniffed and wiped at her eyes. "Poppy wanted to have a bakery just like yours when she grew up. That was her dream, you know, to own a bakery." Marie Claire was staring into space and she didn't answer. She had picked up a little stone bottle of almond essence and was rubbing it between her fingers.

"Maybe," Marie Claire murmured to herself. "If I can remember what went into them. It just might work. Like Proust and his madeleine."

"What are you talking about?" Charlie said, not that she really cared. It was too late now.

"I believe I have one last idea we could try," Marie Claire said softly. "It is a special kind of cake and—"

"We've tried making her things to eat," Charlie cried out. "And it doesn't work. Poppy won't touch anything we give her."

"So that is why," Marie Claire said slowly. "That is why we must give these little cakes to her ourselves. Hand them over, face-to-face, and if she tries one, I believe it just might—"

"You've got to be kidding," Charlie exclaimed, cutting Marie Claire off in midsentence. "She's like a mad person, a crazy girl."

"I know, but what choice do we have?" Marie Claire shrugged. "If we don't try this, then yes, you are right, child, the police will come and take her off to jail."

Back at the patisserie Charlie didn't say a word as she watched Marie Claire mix sugar and almond paste together in her favorite china bowl. She beat in eggs, sifted over flour, and gently stirred in melted butter and a dash of real almond extract. A pinch of salt and then the batter went into the little greased molds shaped like shells.

The smell was intoxicating as the cakes baked, but when they came out of the oven, Charlie was disappointed to see how plain and unfancy they looked.

"Aren't you going to frost those?" she asked, watching Marie Claire pack them into a white paper bag and twist the edges shut.

"No frosting, but we must hurry. I want Poppy to eat one while they are still warm." Charlie didn't ask any more questions, because as they came out of the patisserie, she saw Ms. Roach hurrying down the street toward the shop. Rapidly pulling Marie Claire into an alleyway, Charlie hid there while Ms. Roach banged on the patisserie door, calling out Charlie's name and peering through the glass. Finally, after a few more minutes, the headmistress gave up and left, but her determined, purposeful stride was not exactly comforting.

"She must know I'm with you," Charlie whispered nervously. "It won't be long before she finds us."

"Quickly then," Marie Claire said, cradling the bag of cakes in her hands. "Let us get to Poppy first."

Thankfully, there were no police cars or other vehicles cruising around by the canal. "Should we look in the window and see if she's there?" Charlie whispered.

"No, we shall go straight to the front door and knock," Marie Claire said. "You can come with me, Charlie, but I have to give the cakes to Poppy myself, and you must promise me something," she added sternly.

"What?" Charlie said. Marie Claire looked so serious.

"If anything happens to me, I want you to run straight home. Don't hang around, just go." Marie Claire's voice was strained. "It's important, Charlie. I need to hear you promise."

"I promise," Charlie mumbled, chewing on her nails.

Not surprisingly, there was no answer when they knocked on the door. In fact, no noise came from inside the cottage at all. "Maybe she's gone out again," Charlie whispered, secretly hoping that this might be the case.

"Poppy," Marie Claire called softly. "Are you home,

Poppy?" But her words were left unanswered. The silence was so thick Charlie found it hard to breathe. "I'm going in," Marie Claire mouthed, slowly turning the handle. She pushed open the door, and there, sitting on her packing crate, staring right at them, was Poppy. Her hair hung in long unwashed clumps around her face, and her school uniform was so dirty and ripped it was hard to distinguish the colors. But it was Poppy's eyes that disturbed Charlie the most: those dull, cold eyes that seemed to look right through you without really seeing.

"*Bonjour*, Poppy," Marie Claire said, taking a step toward her. Poppy hunched over, like a snail retreating into its shell. She raised her magic wand in the air. "I've brought you something special," Marie Claire continued in a gentle, singsong voice. "A little treat I made myself."

As she talked, Marie Claire stepped closer, holding out the white paper bag of cakes. "We've missed you, Poppy," she said, and Poppy pushed backward on her packing case, scraping the rough wood across the floor. Now she was pressed up against the far wall with nowhere else to go. A gruntlike moan escaped from Poppy's throat, reminding Charlie of the sound a wounded animal might make. She still held her wand up, as if for protection.

"Here," Marie Claire coaxed, taking a cake from the bag and offering it to Poppy. Her movements were slow and cautious. "Take a taste, *chérie*. It's still warm." Poppy pulled back her arm, and something in her face, perhaps the tensing of her jawline, made Charlie scream.

"No! Please don't. It's me—Charlie."

Ignoring the cry, and showing no emotion whatsoever, Poppy sucked in a mouthful of stale air and started to speak. She got as far as "Consti—" when Marie Claire bravely lunged forward and shoved the little cake in Poppy's mouth. For the first time surprise registered in her expression, and she blinked, as if suddenly realizing there were other people in the room. Charlie and Marie Claire watched as Poppy chewed and swallowed. Then something extraordinary happened. Poppy's arm went slack and she dropped her wand onto the floor. With shaking hands, Poppy picked the remains of the cake out of her lap where it had fallen and took another bite. This time she closed her eyes, and Charlie could see tears leaking out of them. Tears that went on and on, streaming down her face unchecked. Marie Claire crouched down and put an arm around her shoulders. "You are remembering, *chérie*?"

"Yes," Poppy sniffed, opening her eyes and looking at Marie Claire for the first time. "I remember this taste, the feel of the cake in my mouth. I remember being born and you wrapping me up in a warm cloth and how happy I felt. How full and content." She let her tears fall and blinked through them in wonder. "Am I the baby you told me about?"

"You are," Marie Claire said. "You were born right on my patisserie floor in the middle of a beautiful May afternoon. It was a wonderful moment, and the first thing you did was reach out and grab for a bag of these very almond cakes." Marie Claire laughed at the memory, and Charlie laughed too. Not that she understood what was going on. She was just so relieved to hear Poppy's voice again. "So you see," Marie Claire continued, "you were destined to be a cook from the very beginning. I believe you have to be born in a bakery to acquire your kind of passion."

"It's too late now," Poppy croaked, her voice sounding rusty from not being used. "I can't go back. I can't change things. I don't know how."

"Yes, you can," Marie Claire persisted. "And we're here to help you." She settled herself more comfortably on the floor. "Now, don't speak for a moment, please, just listen. I've been doing some serious thinking. My awful old landlord won't renew my lease, but I'm not ready to get out of the bakery business just yet. And you have always wanted to own a cake shop. So here's my idea. This little cottage would make a perfect patisserie. I could live upstairs and you could live with me. If I present your case very carefully to the authorities, I am sure they would agree."

"Oh, Marie Claire, that's a brilliant idea," Charlie cried, hopping about the floor. "I'm so excited, and you know my dad would help out with the carpentry and stuff. He's good at all that kind of thing, and my mum could make curtains and tablecloths."

"No." Poppy shook her head mournfully. "It won't work," she whispered. "I'm a witch. That's why I'm here. I can't ever be anything else."

"Yes, you can," Marie Claire insisted. "You can be whatever you want to be. I was always told that I should study accounting because I was good at math. That's what my nasty old teachers used to say. Well, I hated math. I might have been good at it, but I never enjoyed it. I can imagine nothing worse than sitting in an office all day, staring at numbers."

"It's too late," Poppy said again, her head drooping forward. "No one will believe me. They all think I'm evil. I don't know how to make things right."

"Yes, you do," Marie Claire said. "Otherwise, you wouldn't have remembered being born in my bakery. You are a kind, good person, Poppy. You just need to open up your heart again." She patted Poppy's knee and tucked the bag of almond cakes onto her lap. "All I ask is that you eat up the rest of these cakes. If, when you've finished them, you still feel there is no hope, then we'll leave you in peace. You can live your life as you wish." She sighed. "Turn people to stone, fill yourself up with those revolting Twirlies. But you should know," Marie Claire cautioned, "that the police are looking for you."

"Please go," Poppy whispered, hanging her head still farther so that it was resting on her knees. "I'd like to be alone."

"Come," Marie Claire said, getting up and taking Charlie by the hand.

"No!" Charlie tugged her arm free in dismay. "We can't go. I'm not leaving her."

"There's nothing more we can do," Marie Claire said. "It's up to Poppy now."

"Poppy, please," Charlie begged. "Come with us. Don't stay here by yourself." But Poppy didn't answer. She was as still and immobile as a stone statue. The only sound was the muffled sniff, sniff of someone softly crying.

....

Chapter Twenty-Three

A Visit from the Police

"WAS SHE REALLY BORN IN YOUR BAKERY?" CHARLIE asked as they walked slowly home.

"She was, although I didn't see her again after that, not for ten whole years," Marie Claire said. "Not until she turned up on my doorstep, and that's when I sensed we had met before. Perhaps it was something in her eyes," she remarked, linking her arm through Charlie's. "Eyes are very telling. Of course, I only knew for sure when her parents came storming into my shop to take her back." She glanced down at Charlie and gave a small smile. "You couldn't forget Mr. and Mrs. Pendle in a hurry."

"Do you really believe that's why she loves to cook?"

Charlie asked. "Because she was born in a bakery?"

"Well, it makes sense, don't you think, *chérie*? With a passion like Poppy's, it has to come from somewhere, and she certainly didn't get it from those parents."

"So what will happen now?" Charlie said, feeling her throat constrict and her eyes grow damp.

"We shall just have to wait and see," Marie Claire said rather more briskly than she intended. It was hard not to notice just how many trees in Potts Bottom had stone birds perched in their branches.

When Charlie got home, her parents met her at the door, both of them looking worried. "Charlie, this is getting out of hand," her father said straightaway. "It's time you talked to the police."

"I'm quite sure they'll be round here soon enough anyway," Mrs. Monroe added. "By now that headmistress from Ruthersfield will certainly have told them you know where Poppy is."

"I'll have to hide," Charlie yawned, suddenly feeling exhausted. "Don't tell them I'm here, please, Mum."

"We have to," Mrs. Monroe stressed. "This is the police, Charlie. We can't conceal your whereabouts."

"Yes, you can. I'm your daughter." And crawling under the sitting room sofa, Charlie curled up into a tight ball and fell asleep.

It was a flashlight shining in her face that woke her up. "Come out of there please, miss," an official-sounding voice said. Charlie blinked, staring into the spotty face of a policeman. He didn't look much older than Charlie herself. She squeezed her eyes shut and lay still for a few moments, hoping he might go away. Unfortunately, he didn't, and when Charlie peeked again, he was still on his hands and knees, watching her.

"We'd just like to ask you a few questions, miss."

"Don't worry, Charlie. You're not in any trouble," her mother reassured her as Charlie crawled out from under the sofa.

"You just need to tell us where Poppy is," a second policeman, who looked almost as young as the first, said. The spotty policeman flipped open a notebook and cleared his throat.

"Can you tell us where Poppy Pendle might be hiding?" he questioned, his face reminding Charlie of a large cheese pizza.

"I'm a bit thirsty," Charlie said, trying to stall for time. "Do you mind if I just get a drink of water?" The policeman nodded his permission, and Charlie hurried into the kitchen. As she stood at the sink, filling a glass with water, she glanced out of the window and saw that her goose had moved again. He wasn't standing under the apple tree, and she looked around the garden, searching to see where he had settled. Charlie leaned forward and opened the window, hitching herself up on the sink and peering farther out. She shrieked in surprise because there was her goose, directly beneath her. Only he wasn't made of stone anymore. Soft, smooth white feathers covered his body. At the sound of her voice, the goose tilted his head up and looked right at Charlie out of inquisitive brown eyes. He ruffled his feathers, gave a little nod with his beak, and waddled back across the garden. That's when Charlie felt a large, sweaty hand grip her shoulder, and the spotty officer's voice said, "Don't try to escape."

"I'm not," Charlie said truthfully, still staring at her goose. She couldn't quite believe he was real, and if he was real, she couldn't quite believe what this meant. Poppy had reversed the Stop It Now Spell! She was back from the dark side, and Charlie smothered a soft squeal. "I just needed a little air," she confessed, shivering with excitement. "It's awfully hot in here, don't you think?"

"Get down, please," the officer ordered, escorting Charlie off the sink. He held her firmly by the arm and led her back into the living room.

"Charlie, really!" her mother admonished. "You'll just make matters worse. Please cooperate."

"Yes, Mum," Charlie said, smiling at the policeman, whose name was PC Plunket, according to his shiny brass badge.

"So where is Poppy Pendle?" PC Plunket asked again, pencil poised above his notebook. "We have been informed by Ms. Roach that you know of her whereabouts."

"That's right," Charlie agreed. "I do. Is Poppy in trouble?" she asked innocently.

"You mustn't pretend, Charlie," her mother said. "The police know everything."

"Oh?" Charlie attempted to look puzzled. "What's she done?" Charlie asked, stalling for time.

"Don't play games, young lady," PC Plunket commanded, holding up his hand for silence. "Miss Pendle has been charged with turning six individuals to stone," he announced gravely. "She is also under suspicion for the disappearance of PC Flower. These are serious offenses, and a warrant has been issued for her arrest." He gave Charlie a hard stare. "Poppy Pendle is an extremely dangerous young woman, and we need to find her as quickly as possible before any more crimes are committed." Charlie smothered a laugh and skipped over to the door. PC Plunket was right behind her. "Stop right there, Miss Monroe," he barked. "You do not leave these premises."

"I was just going to take you to Poppy's," Charlie said, looking up at PC Plunket out of wide, innocent eyes. "Only I'm terrible at giving directions, so I thought I'd show you the way myself."

"Did you now?" PC Plunket thought hard for a moment, trying to see where the catch in this suggestion was. He frowned and scratched his spotty chin. "Very well," he agreed at last. Then as an afterthought he added, "But you've got to hold on to my hand, because I'll not have you running off again."

"We'll come too, if that's all right with you, Constable?" Mr. Monroe said.

"Dad, there's really no need." Charlie smiled at her father and winked. "Everything's under control."

Chapter Twenty-Four

....

The Return of Poppy Pendle

THERE SEEMED TO BE AN AWFUL LOT OF BIRDS THAT were fluttering about town. The air was full of singing, and Charlie noticed that all the birds on the telephone wire were now hopping about in a delirious frenzy.

"You would think it was the first day of spring," PC Plunket's partner commented. His name was PC Nobs, and he kept staring about in bewilderment. "Something seems different," he said in a puzzled tone, "but I can't put my finger on it." A cat darted out in front of them, chasing its tail in circles. Squirrels raced up and down trees, and a family of ducks flapped about the sky as if they couldn't decide in which direction to fly.

Charlie, holding on to PC Plunket's warm, sweaty hand, led the police officers straight to Marie Claire's patisserie. She walked fast because it was embarrassing, holding hands with a policeman, and she didn't want anyone to see her. "She's in here?" PC Plunket said in disbelief. "You know, harboring a fugitive is a serious offense."

"Oh no," Charlie giggled, shaking back her frizzy mass of hair. "I just wanted to bring Marie Claire along with us. She's a close friend of Poppy's too."

"We've been trying to get ahold of Ms. Marie Claire Gentille for questioning too," PC Plunket remarked, banging on the glass door. He gave Charlie a suspicious look. "It seems you both know rather a lot about Poppy Pendle."

Marie Claire was happy to accompany the police officers and Charlie. Especially when Charlie mouthed the word "Goose!" at her and scrunched up her face in what was clearly an expression of joy. Marie Claire even agreed to hold PC Plunket's other hand. "What a beautiful day it is," she declared, exchanging knowing smiles with Charlie. "The birds seem awfully cheerful."

"That's just what I was saying," PC Nobs agreed eagerly. "I wonder what's making them so noisy?"

"Well now, will you look at that," PC Plunket exclaimed, coming to an abrupt stop as they reached the top of the canal path. Shining in the sun, all white enamel and polished chrome, was the oven. "Who would throw away a cooker like that?" he asked. "It looks like it's in excellent condition."

"Peculiar," PC Nobs agreed, scratching at his head.

"It's more than peculiar. It's downright suspicious, and look at all this food," PC Plunket remarked. "Bags of flour and sugar, bars of chocolate. Eggs." He grimaced after stepping on a dozen. "I'll get to the bottom of this later," he said, wiping gooey yolk off the bottoms of his shoes. "I hope you know where you're leading me, Miss Monroe, because we don't have all day to waste marching about the countryside."

"Right there," Charlie said, pointing at the abandoned cottage. Except it didn't look all that abandoned. Smoke was coming out of the chimney, and the yard appeared to be swarming with animals. A red-tailed fox was lying in the sun, and grazing beside it was a speckled roe deer. Rabbits and squirrels darted about in the long grass, and perched on all the tree branches were noisily singing birds. Even the canal was busier than usual as a family of ducks and two regal swans floated by.

"Are you sure Miss Pendle's inside?" PC Plunket asked. "I believe this area's been searched already."

"Absolutely certain," Charlie confirmed. "I saw her just yesterday."

"Then I ask you all to stand back, please, because she's armed and dangerous. This is a matter for the police." PC Plunket clambered over the stone wall and stood with his shoulders pulled back, surveying the cottage. "Get down!" he suddenly yelled, grabbing for his truncheon as a rustling noise came from behind the holly bush. Out crawled PC Flower, looking dazed and slightly sick. He stood up and stumbled around, as if he'd just gotten off a spinning ride at the fair. "She's in there. I've f-f-f-found her," he stammered.

"Flower, are you all right?" PC Plunket called out. "What on earth is going on? Where have you been, man?" He glanced back at Charlie and Marie Claire as if they might have an answer, but the two of them simply shrugged.

"Wild, crazy eyes," PC Flower wailed softly, picking a holly leaf out of his hair. "She's insane. She's t-t-t-t-terrifying. We need more reinforcements."

And that's when the front door was flung open, sending PC Flower scurrying back behind the holly bush with a panicked cry. "You're under arrest," PC Plunket shouted bravely, huddling down in the tall grass.

"I thought I heard voices," Poppy Pendle called out,

leaning against a broomstick. Her hair hung in two tidy braids, and her face had been scrubbed so clean it was as pink and polished as a rosy apple. Poppy's eyes sparkled. "I was just making crepes in the fireplace if anyone would care to join me."

"You're under arrest," PC Plunket repeated, scrambling up and marching toward the house. PC Nobs followed him. "We're coming in."

"Yes, please do," Poppy said, waving at Charlie and Marie Claire. "Everyone's invited. And I'm so sorry I scared you," Poppy said, putting her hands on her knees and calling over to the holly bush. "I honestly didn't know what I was doing. Please come out and have some crepes, won't you?" PC Flower's face appeared, looking more perplexed than ever. He gave a frantic shake of his head and darted quickly out of sight.

"Hand over the broomstick," PC Plunket instructed, holding his truncheon aloft as he stepped inside the cottage. "And no funny business."

"It doesn't sweep very well, I'm afraid," Poppy apologized. "But you're welcome to have it. I only wanted to tidy up in here, but the bristles aren't really designed for sweeping."

"This will be held as evidence," PC Plunket said, "and you no longer have a license to fly. Your learning permit has been canceled."

"Really? That's great." Poppy looked pleased. "You mean I never have to get on a broomstick again?"

"Magic wand as well, please," PC Plunket barked. "From this moment on you are not, under Yorkshire law, allowed to practice witchcraft."

"Hurray!" Poppy shouted, tossing the spotty-faced policeman her magic wand. "What happens if someone tries to make me?" she added as an afterthought. "What if I'm given a new wand?"

"You are banned from the practice of magic forever," PC Plunket said in his gravest voice.

"Yay! I'm free," Poppy cried out, skipping over to Charlie and Marie Claire, who were wandering around the cottage in amazement. All the cans and Twirlie bar wrappers had been swept into a corner, and a small fire was burning in the hearth. On top of it rested a wide, flat stone, and beside the fireplace was a glass measuring jug of thick, creamy batter.

"Miss, are you Poppy Pendle?" PC Plunket seemed confused. "Poppy Pendle of Ten Pudding Lane?" He was opening and closing a pair of handcuffs as if he didn't quite know what to do with them.

"Yes, that's me," Poppy answered.

"Then hold out your hands because you're under arrest." Just at that moment PC Plunket's telephone started to ring, and he patted his pockets in a fluster, trying to find it. "PC Plunket speaking," he said a little breathlessly. "Oh yes, sir, we have, sir. I'll be bringing her in shortly. And we've recovered PC Flower, safe and sound. It appears he's had some sort of nasty shock, but I can't get much out of him. A nice hot bath and some chicken soup should do the trick." There was a long pause on PC Plunket's end while he listened at length to whatever the other person had to say. When he hung up, he looked even more confused. "That was Officer Kibble," he announced. "It appears that PC Crud and PC Nuttle are no longer made of stone."

"Fantastic!" Marie Claire and Charlie shrieked together, throwing themselves on Poppy.

"I knew you could do it," Marie Claire whispered, squeezing both girls in a tight hug.

"What about the workers at Super Savers?" PC Nobs inquired. "The stock boy and the manager?"

"All back to normal. Although"—and here PC Plunket lowered his voice a notch—"it seems Mrs. Smegs, the manager's wife, is not too happy about that. She told Officer Kibble she preferred her husband being stone. Much easier to take care of, apparently."

"So you won't be needing those," Marie Claire said, pointing at the handcuffs that PC Plunket was still playing with. "I mean, you can't arrest Poppy for a crime that doesn't exist anymore."

"Mmmm." PC Plunket pondered this for a moment, and then he said gruffly, "There's still the matter of stolen food." He pulled out his notebook and flipped over a few pages. "Eighteen cans of mystery meat stew, twenty-four boxes of Twirlies, and thirty-two packets of Fudge Monkeys."

"That was me, I'm afraid," Poppy confessed. "And when you put it like that, I'm just horrified. Was it really thirty-two packets of Fudge Monkeys?"

"Thirty-two," PC Plunket repeated, snapping his notebook closed.

"It appears all the evidence is over there," PC Nobs added, nodding at the pile of rubbish Poppy had swept into the corner.

"Well, that is certainly a terrible crime I've committed," Poppy agreed. "Anyone who eats twenty-four boxes of Twirlies and thirty-two packets of Fudge Monkeys should be locked up for life. I've no defense, I'm afraid, except to say I must have been out of my mind."

"You were out of your mind," Marie Claire defended stoutly, "but if you repay the store for the food you took, it is not a jail sentence." She glared at PC Plunket.

"Oh, I'll give it all back to Super Savers, every penny," Poppy reassured him. "Only it might take me a while to get my bakery up and running."

"You're really going to start a bakery?" Charlie said, her cheeks flushing pink with excitement.

"If Marie Claire is serious about living here with me," Poppy said, cutting a shy glance in her direction. "I can't do this alone."

"You don't have to," Marie Claire whispered, and her eyes glistened brightly with tears. "You don't have to."

"There is the small matter of Mr. and Mrs. Pendle," PC Plunket mentioned, picking at one of his spots. "Poppy is a minor and she cannot leave home without their permission."

"Then I will get it," Marie Claire said boldly. "I shall sort this all out so everything is legal. Don't you worry, Officer Plunket."

"And what about school?" PC Plunket asked.

"Oh no," Poppy groaned. "I can't bear it. Just the thought of Ruthersfield makes me feel sick. I never want to go back there again."

"You don't have to," PC Plunket informed her. "You've been expelled, I'm afraid. In fact, Ms. Roach has requested that you never set foot on the academy grounds again.

"Yaaaay!" Poppy and Charlie screamed, hugging each other and jumping up and down.

"Which still leaves the question of schooling. You

are very much a minor, Miss Pendle, and some sort of education will be required."

"Can I go to the elementary school with Charlie?" Poppy suggested. "I could bake in the afternoons and help out on weekends until I'm old enough to take over."

"That seems like an excellent arrangement," Marie Claire said, trying to hustle the policemen out of the cottage. "So is there anything left to discuss?"

"I do have one last question." PC Plunket shuffled his boots about in embarrassment. "Will you be selling those chocolate cookies that melt in your mouth when you open your new bakery?" His face blushed tomato-sauce red. "I loved those cookies," he sighed, closing his eyes for a moment. "You made them once at Patisserie Marie Claire."

"I didn't make them," Marie Claire explained. "Poppy did, so you will have to ask her."

"Thursdays," Poppy said with a smile. "I shall make them every Thursday." And PC Plunket looked delighted.

"Those were the best-tasting cookies I ever had," he admitted. "They cheered me right up, even after Officer Kibble had been shouting his head off at all of us." PC Plunket fiddled with his badge for a moment, then said, "If you ever want my mum's brownie recipe,

I'm sure she'd give it to you. They're the fudgy kind. She makes them when it rains as a bit of a treat."

"Oh, that would be lovely," Poppy said. "There's nothing nicer than a good squidgy brownie."

Poppy asked if the policemen wanted to stay for crepes, but they said they had better be going. "More criminals to catch," PC Plunket joked, winking at Poppy. "And I'd better get poor old PC Flower home." He waved her magic wand in the air and said, "How do you use this thing, anyway?"

"You can't unless you're magic."

"Won't you miss it at all?" PC Plunket couldn't help asking.

"Nope." Poppy gave a decisive shake of her head. "Flying on a broomstick makes me feel sick, and I'd much rather make cookies than potions." She gave PC Plunket the full benefit of her most dazzling smile. "This is the happiest day of my life so far," Poppy told him. "And it's only just begun."

Chapter Twenty-Five

....

A Bit of a Stony Problem

THE LITTLE TERRACE HOUSE ON PUDDING LANE HAD A sad, abandoned look about it. Weeds had overtaken the front garden, and the milkman obviously hadn't been getting the message that no one was home. There were about thirty full milk bottles clustered around the doorstep. Marie Claire gave a brisk knock on the front door, but after she'd waited a while and knocked again, it was clear that no one was going to answer.

"Perhaps we should just leave," Poppy said. "They obviously don't want to see me. I've let them down, and they're never going to forgive me."

"Well, they're in," Marie Claire pointed out. "I can

see them through the kitchen window. Poppy followed Marie Claire's gaze and felt her knees go weak and start to buckle. That was just how she had left them.

"Please, let's go," Poppy pleaded, but it was too late. Nosy old Maxine from next door was trotting eagerly up the path. She had on bedroom slippers, a dressing gown, and her hair was full of rollers.

"The police are looking for you," she exclaimed, gasping for breath, but before she could utter another word, Marie Claire smoothly broke in.

"Everything's under control now, so if you would be kind enough to open the door for us."

"You're in a great deal of trouble, Poppy Pendle. A great deal."

"All sorted out actually," Marie Claire said. "I suggest you go and call the police station. They'll be able to give you the details. Ask to speak to PC Plunket. He's in charge of this case."

"I know who PC Plunket is," Maxine said suspiciously, getting out her key and opening the Pendles' front door. She was about to step inside, but Marie Claire slipped by her fast and stood in the doorway, her arms folded across her chest.

"Thank you. That will be all." With an aggrieved sniff, Maxine spun around and marched off down the path.

"I'll be calling PC Plunket right away," she threatened. "So let's hope what you've told me is true."

"Come on," Marie Claire whispered, reaching for Poppy's hand. "That woman is an old busybody. Let's get this over with before she comes back."

The house was too quiet, and Poppy sensed, even before she entered the kitchen, what they would find. *"Mon Dieu!"* Marie Claire cried out softly, staring at the two stone figures. "They have not changed back." She turned to look at Poppy, as if searching for an answer. "How can this be?"

"I don't know." Poppy gave a nervous shrug.

"But everyone else is just fine," Marie Claire murmured, stepping up to Mrs. Pendle and touching her stone hand. "Perhaps you are still angry with them?" she suggested. "Perhaps you had more fury behind this particular spell than the others?"

"I'm not angry anymore," Poppy whispered, putting her arms around her father's waist. It was so much easier being with her parents when they couldn't talk back. She looked over at her mother's anguished face, full of pain and heartache, and Poppy wished that she hadn't disappointed them so. Life would have been completely different if only she'd wanted to be a witch. "Maybe they're still mad at me," Poppy said. "What about that, Marie Claire? Perhaps *they* have to stop being angry as well?"

"I don't know," Marie Claire sighed. "I just don't know, but the question is, what shall we do with them both? We really can't leave them here. It doesn't seem right."

"No, and they are still my parents," Poppy acknowledged, trying not to look at the space where the oven used to be. She could feel herself starting to get mad again. Taking a deep, calming breath, Poppy said, "Let's bring them with us. That solves the problem, doesn't it? They can come live in the cottage, or outside might be better," she added quickly. "The cottage is rather small."

"Yes." Marie Claire nodded her approval. "We'll find just the right spot for Edith and Roger, and I'm sure Charlie's father would be happy to give them a ride over in his truck."

"Oh, he doesn't need to do that." Poppy grinned. "I can carry my mum and dad."

"They're solid stone," Marie Claire pointed out. "You couldn't possibly lift one of these, let alone two."

"Watch me," Poppy said, picking up Roger under one arm and Edith under the other. She could see through the window that nosy old Maxine was hovering about in her front garden, raking up some nonexistent leaves and glancing over at their house every few seconds. Poppy hesitated a moment and then headed toward the back door. "It might be better if we go out this way," she suggested, hitching Edith up a bit and trying not to let her slip. It was hard to keep a good grip around her mother's waist.

Thank goodness it was a Sunday afternoon and most of Potts Bottom's residents were either slumped in front of their televisions watching football or finishing up Sunday lunch. The streets were deserted, and a powerful smell of roast meat hung in the air.

"Careful," Marie Claire said, steadying Poppy as she tripped and stumbled forward, almost dropping her parents on the ground. "You don't want them to break, now."

"No, that wouldn't be a good idea," Poppy agreed, slowing down her pace. Her shirt had come untucked and she could feel her socks slipping, but it was hard not to skip when she felt so happy.

"Have you always been this strong?" Marie Claire said.

"Ever since I was a baby." Poppy grinned. "Must have been the almond cakes you gave me when I was born."

"Well, those are good, but they're certainly not full of any special powers." Marie Claire laughed. "My guess is that sort of strength comes from being magic."

"Yes," Poppy sighed wistfully. "They can take away my wand and broomstick, but they can't take away my magic."

"You shouldn't want them to," Marie Claire said with force. "It's a part of who you are. A big part. That's what makes you, you," she said, stabbing at the air with her finger. Poppy opened her mouth to say something, but Marie Claire hurried on. "We can't change who we are, Poppy, but we can choose what we do."

Poppy thought about this for a moment, and then shaking back a clump of hair, she burst out, "Well, I choose to be a baker." It sounded so good that she said it again and then again, shouting the words louder and louder each time. "I CHOOSE TO BE A BAKER."

"Good choice." Marie Claire smiled. "Really good choice!"

Chapter Twenty-Six

....

Happily Ever After

POPPY'S OPENED FOR BUSINESS ON MAY 3, THE DAY Poppy turned eleven. It had taken almost a year to renovate the bakery, but it was the best birthday present Poppy had ever had. Marie Claire moved out of the patisserie and for an embarrassingly small sum of money had purchased the little cottage down by the canal. With a great deal of help from PC Plunket (who couldn't wait for the bakery to open), Charlie's dad had put on a new roof and replaced all the windows. In fact, PC Plunket proved to be excellent with a hammer. He hung drywall, built a new set of stairs, and in return Poppy promised to save him a dozen chocolate melt-aways every Thursday.

Best of all, PC Plunket tactfully didn't mention the fact that two life-size stone statues looking remarkably like Edith and Roger Pendle had been positioned on either side of the bakery's front door. It was clear that Poppy Pendle had come back from the dark side, so why make a fuss? That was most people's opinion. Even Auntie Viv didn't seem to mind. She and nosy old Maxine drank coffee and gossiped together now most mornings, ever since Viv had moved into the house on Pudding Lane. It did seem a shame to waste all that lovely space with no one living there anymore, and her little flat was the size of a postage stamp.

So life unfolded into a comforting routine, and one that Poppy looked forward to from the moment she woke up. While Marie Claire was still sleeping, Poppy would start the bread doughs and croissants. She loved the quiet of early morning and the peace and tranquillity of the canal drifting by. Soon the little kitchen would be filled with the sweet, yeasty scent of baking, and when the wind was blowing from the south, people claimed to be able to smell Poppy's fresh breads right across town. There was always a line waiting outside the bakery before it even opened, and visitors to Potts Bottom often asked for directions to the place that smelled so good.

Every morning before leaving the bakery, Poppy

would hang an OPEN sign around her father's neck and bid him a cheery hello. He always looked back at her with the same startled expression, as if he had just seen something unbelievable. She liked to tell her parents what the day's specials were, just to keep them involved, and she was sure that on coconut cupcake Mondays the corners of her father's mouth sometimes twitched. Then, with a bright smile and a wave to Marie Claire, Poppy would skip off to meet the school bus.

At six o'clock, when the bakery shut for the evening, Poppy hung the closed sign around her mother's neck, trying to avoid looking too closely at the tragic stone face. There was something rather disturbing about her angry, bug-eyed stare, and the enormous mouthful of food Edith Pendle still appeared to be chewing.

Charlie spent as much time visiting Poppy's as she could, but she liked to get home before dark to feed her goose. He had made a permanent home under the old apple tree in Charlie's garden and continued to be an excellent eater, gulping down muffins and gingerbread and even the odd grilled cheese sandwich. Sometimes when Charlie walked down to the bakery, her goose would waddle along behind. While she helped serve customers or watched Poppy invent a new cookie recipe, her goose would go for a quick swim in the canal.

As soon as he saw Charlie wave good-bye, though, he flapped out of the water, gave his feathers a brisk shake, and scuttled after her with a series of excited honks.

One Wednesday, a few months after the bakery had opened, Ms. Roach appeared in the shop. Ducking down behind the counter, Poppy held her breath and hoped that she hadn't been seen. "Hello, Poppy," Ms. Roach greeted loudly, and Poppy scrambled to her feet with a sheepish smile. "I see you have some nice stone artwork out front," she said, and before Poppy could answer, she pointed to the last ten caramel cookies. "I'll take all of those, please."

"Yes, Ms. Roach," Poppy mumbled, putting the cookies into a box. She waited for Ms. Roach to say something more, but the headmistress didn't. She took her cookies and left. The next week though, an order came in from Ruthersfield Academy for ten dozen caramel cookies to be delivered to the school every Wednesday. At the bottom of the order was a note from Ms. Roach. It said, "Those were the best cookies I have ever eaten. Your great-grandmother Mabel was a wonderful witch, and you are a wonderful baker."

And Poppy's parents? Well, they stood outside the shop for two whole years, watching the people of

Potts Bottom come and go. There was always a steady stream of customers to look at, and sometimes people would greet them by name. "Hello, Edith," or "How's it going, Roger," they'd call out, giving the stone statues a friendly pat on their tummies. In the winter months Poppy dressed her parents in woolly hats and scarves, and they became a popular target for snowball-throwing practice.

As soon as the weather turned nice, Poppy liked to sit on the steps between them, munching chocolate croissants and chattering away about new recipe ideas. On Poppy's thirteenth birthday, when she went outside to hang the OPEN sign around her dad's neck, she was surprised to notice that he blinked. That was all at first, a blink here, a blink there, and then his mouth started to move. The first thing he said was, "I'm hungry," so Poppy fed him warm pieces of chocolate butter bread, and it wasn't long after that, that he began to move. He was more than a little stiff to begin with, but Poppy greased his joints with the best Normandy butter and quite soon he was parading about with an enormous smile plastered across his face.

"I'm sorry about Mum," Poppy apologized to her dad, because Edith Pendle was still as cold and hard as a Yorkshire paving stone.

"Oh, she'll come around," Roger Pendle said brightly,

and she did. But it took her another two years. It was Poppy's fifteenth birthday when Edith Pendle finally opened her mouth and spat out the remains of a Twirlie bar. "Ugh!" She grimaced. "That tastes disgusting."

"Mum!" Poppy cried out, giving Edith Pendle a hug. She was still a little cold and hard to the touch, but Poppy could feel her mother's heart beating away.

"Be a love, Poppy, and whip up a batch of those fabulous homemade Twirlies you bake on Mondays, would you?" Edith Pendle smiled at her daughter and added, "I see now you were born to be a baker."

Poppy was happy to oblige, and the rest, as they say, is history.

Poppy lived all her life in the little cottage bakery down by the canal. The picture of Great-Granny Mabel was moved from the house on Pudding Lane and hung on the shop wall above the counter, right next to Poppy's Baker of the Year award. Every time her parents ate something that Poppy had made, they would close their eyes and sigh, then point at the photo and say, "Your great-granny Mabel would have been so proud of you."

Occasionally when Poppy had created something especially fabulous, she would get so excited that fireworks would explode out of the bowl. Or perhaps a bouquet of rainbow-colored balloons would appear in the oven along with her latest creation. Whenever this happened, Poppy simply smiled and gave a shrug, because she really didn't mind being magic, just so long as she could keep on baking.

Simple Baking Tips from Poppy's Bakery

. . . .

1. Always wash your hands before you begin baking.

2. Ask an adult for permission and/or to help you to set up and use kitchen equipment, crack eggs, cut with knives, or take pans in and out of the oven, etc.

3. Good ingredients make the best cakes and cookies. Nothing is better than butter!

4. All the cookie recipes can be easily halved if you don't want to make a full batch.

5. Measure your flour by gently scooping it out. Don't pack the flour down, and always level off your measuring cups and spoons. A simple way to do this is to draw the back of a knife across the top, swiping away any excess flour.

6. Poppy recommends using kosher salt in all her recipes. If you are using regular salt, you might want to use a little less.

7. When a recipe calls for eggs, use large, not extra large, and make sure they are at room temperature. Just leave them out on the counter for an hour before you start to bake.

8. You might want to use an oven thermometer to make sure your oven is cooking at the correct temperature. Sometimes ovens will run hotter or cooler than the

temperature they have been set at, and it's good to know this before starting to bake.

9. A rubber spatula is an extremely useful cooking tool that has a rubber head. It's the best tool to use for scraping bowls clean and getting batter into pans. Most kitchens have at least one!

10. It's a good idea to wash up your sticky bowls and pans, and put away ingredients when you have finished baking. If you do this, the adults in your house will be much more likely to let you use the kitchen again. They tend to get a little cranky (and rightly so!) if you leave them all your cleaning up.

11. And the most important rule of all: Have fun and enjoy sharing your goodies with your family and friends. If your cakes sink or your cookies are a little too crispy, it's okay. They will still taste delicious, and the only way to get better is to keep practicing.

Recipes

* * *

Poppy's Famous Chocolate Melt-Aways

Makes about 50 melt-aways

These are just as delicious as they sound. One bite and they literally melt away on the tongue. Full of butter and good dark cocoa, they are a chocolate lover's dream. If you don't mind them crumbling a bit, sandwich some softened vanilla ice cream between two melt-aways for an extra special treat.

~ INGREDIENTS ~

1 cup (2 sticks) butter, softened

½ cup sugar

1⅔ cups self-rising flour (or all-purpose flour with a teaspoon of baking powder mixed in)

½ cup plus 1 tablespoon unsweetened cocoa powder (NOT hot cocoa mix)

¼ teaspoon salt

2 teaspoons vanilla extract

~ Method ~

. . . .

1. Preheat the oven to 350°F.

2. Make sure your butter is really soft—this is important;
    otherwise, the ingredients won't blend together smoothly.
    The best way to soften butter is to leave it out of the
    fridge overnight so it comes to room temperature. You
    can soften it in the microwave for a few seconds, but
    be very careful not to melt it. You want soft butter, not
    melted butter!

3. If you have a food processor or standing mixer, just dump
    in all the ingredients and mix everything up together.
    Then go directly to step 5. If not, a handheld mixer will
    work just fine. You might want to ask an adult to help
    you set up your equipment.

4. Put the softened butter and sugar into a large bowl, and
    using a handheld mixer, beat them together until light
    and fluffy. Then add the flour, cocoa powder, salt, and
    vanilla. Go slowly at first; otherwise, the dry ingredients
    will fly out of the bowl! As the mixture comes together,
    speed up beating until you have a soft, slightly sticky
    dough.

5. This is the fun part! Make sure your hands are clean and
    dry. Have ready two cookie pans (flat baking sheets).
    Using about 1 heaping teaspoon of the dough for each,
    roll the mixture into small balls, and put the balls onto the

baking sheets. Don't put them too close together, because you will flatten them out in a minute. Your hands will get all gooey, but they will taste delicious!

6. Wash your hands! Now take a fork and stick it briefly into a glass of water. Then flatten the cookie with the underside of the fork, pressing the tines gently into each ball to spread it out. You will need to wet the fork every four or five cookies to stop it from sticking to the dough.

7. When all the cookies have been flattened, bake for about 18 to 22 minutes. It is hard to tell when these cookies are done because they are such a dark color to begin with. What you are aiming for is a crisp, melting cookie with deep chocolate flavor. Some ovens run hotter than others, so you might want to bake a small batch first and see how long they need. Let them cool completely and then try one. They will crisp up as they cool. If the first batch is not quite crisp enough, bake the next tray a little longer. If the cookies have a slightly burnt taste, you have left them in too long, so take a few minutes off the next round. It is worth getting these cookies perfect because they are so delicious!

8. Store the chocolate melt-aways at room temperature in an airtight container.

Caramel Crunch Cookies

Makes about 50 caramel crunch cookies

Poppy invented these cookies her first morning at Marie Claire's bakery. They quickly became a favorite with the customers and always sell out early. Like the chocolate melt-aways, these are delicious sandwiched together with vanilla ice cream.

~ INGREDIENTS ~

1½ cups all-purpose flour

¼ cup cornstarch

⅔ cup dark brown sugar (This gives the lovely caramel flavor, so use the darkest, stickiest brown sugar you can find. Light brown sugar won't be intense enough.)

½ teaspoon salt

1 cup (2 sticks) butter, softened

2 teaspoons vanilla extract

GLAZE:

1 egg white, beaten, blended with 1 tablespoon water

Raw sugar (sometimes called Turbinado sugar, which has bigger crystals for more crunch)

~ METHOD ~

· ·

1. Preheat the oven to 300°F.

2. You can stir this dough by hand or in a food processor
    or standing mixer. If you are using a food processor or
    standing mixer, simply put in all the ingredients (except
    the glaze) and mix until blended. Then go directly to step 5.

3. Otherwise, whisk together the flour, cornstarch, brown
    sugar, and salt in a large bowl.

4. Cut the butter into pieces, and add it to the bowl. Mash
    with the back of a fork to blend it in, or rub the butter
    into the dry ingredients using your fingertips. At first
    the mixture will look like dry crumbs, but as you work
    the butter into smaller and smaller pieces, the dough will
    begin to get sticky. Now pour in the vanilla. You can
    use a fork to mix it in or your fingers. This is when you
    squish the whole lot together until it forms a large ball.

5. Get out two cookie pans (flat baking sheets). If you only
    have one, that's fine. You can bake the cookies in batches.
    Break off pieces of dough and roll them into small balls,
    about 1 heaping teaspoonful each. Place the cookie balls
    on the baking sheets. Then, using the heel of your hand
    or the tips of your fingers, press down gently on each
    ball to flatten it out slightly. You don't want them too flat
    because they will spread in the oven. Try to make sure
    they are all an even thickness, about ¼ inch.

6. Brush the top of each cookie lightly with the glaze, and sprinkle with the raw sugar. If you like, you can stick a sliver of pecan on top for decoration.

7. Bake cookies for about 35 minutes, until deep golden. You might want to ask an adult to help you get the cookies into and out of the oven. It's a good idea to turn the pans around halfway through cooking so the cookies bake evenly. The low oven temperature is what gives these cookies their delicious caramel crunch. A lovely buttery caramel scent will waft from your oven, telling you the cookies are done.

8. Cool on wire racks, and store in an airtight container to keep them crunchy.

Raspberry Jam Shortbreads

Makes about 70 little shortbread cookies

These cookies look like precious jewels, with their shimmering raspberry jam centers. Poppy likes to arrange them on antique wooden trays and display them in the window of her bakery.

~ INGREDIENTS ~

1 cup (2 sticks) butter, softened

½ cup plus 3 tablespoons confectioners' sugar

2 teaspoons vanilla extract

½ teaspoon salt

1¾ cups flour

¼ cup cornstarch

Raspberry jam

~ METHOD ~

1. Preheat the oven to 350°F.
2. You can make these in a food processor or a standing

mixer if you like. Just ask an adult to help you set up your equipment. Then simply dump in all the ingredients EXCEPT the raspberry jam! Mix well to form a soft dough, and go directly to step 4.

3. Otherwise, put the butter in a large mixing bowl. Make sure it's nice and soft. Add the confectioners' sugar. Using a handheld mixer, beat the butter and sugar together. Now mix in the vanilla extract. Add the salt, flour, and cornstarch, and blend it all together.

4. Place the bowl of cookie dough in the fridge, and chill it for about 15 minutes.

5. Scoop out teaspoonful-size nuggets of cookie dough and roll them into balls. Place the balls on cookie pans (flat baking sheets), leaving a little room between the cookies.

6. Now dip your thumb in flour and make a nice wide thumbprint in the center of each cookie. Pat your thumb around. What you are aiming for is a wide, shallow indent with a thin border of dough around the outside. This is so you will have plenty of room for the jam.

7. Take a little scoop of jam (use the ¼ teaspoon measuring spoon) and fill the middle of the cookie with delicious raspberry jam.

8. Put the tray of filled cookies back in the fridge to chill, for about 10 minutes.

9. Bake the cookies for 18 to 21 minutes, or until the outside

crust is a light golden color. You might want to ask an adult to help you get the cookies into and out of the oven.

10. Cool the cookies on a wire tray. Store at room temperature in an airtight container. These cookies also freeze well.

Coconut Cupcakes

These are absolutely delicious! They are moist, coco-nutty sponge cakes covered in creamy frosting, with a crunch of toasted coconut flakes sprinkled on top. They are Mr. Pendle's favorite.

~ INGREDIENTS ~

1⅓ cups all-purpose flour

½ teaspoon baking powder

¼ teaspoon baking soda

¼ teaspoon salt

½ cup (1 stick) butter, softened

¾ cup sugar

2 large eggs

1 teaspoon vanilla extract

¾ cup unsweetened coconut milk

1 cup shredded, sweetened coconut

~ METHOD ~

. . . .

1. Preheat the oven to 325°F.

2. In a medium bowl, sift together the flour, baking powder, baking soda, and salt.

3. Now put the butter and sugar into another bowl. You can do this in a standing mixer (ask an adult to help you set it up) or use a handheld mixer. Cream together the butter and sugar until light and fluffy. ("Cream" is a fancy word for beat or mix.)

4. Add the eggs one at a time, mixing in well. Then add the vanilla.

5. Now take turns adding some of the flour mixture, some of the coconut milk, some of the flour mixture, some of the coconut milk, and so on until they have both been used up. Gently stir in the shredded coconut.

6. Line 14 to 16 muffin molds with paper cupcake wrappers and pour in the batter, about ½ to ⅔ full, depending on how big you like your cupcakes. Bake for 22 to 28 minutes, until very light golden and spongy. (When you press the top gently, it will bounce back.) There should be no liquid visible. Remove from the tin and cool on a wire rack.

7. Frost with Coconut Buttercream Frosting when cool.

Coconut Buttercream Frosting

~ Ingredients ~

. . . .

½ cup shredded, sweetened coconut

½ cup (1 stick) butter, softened

1¼ cups powdered sugar

1 teaspoon vanilla extract

2 tablespoons coconut milk, or more, to mix

~ Method ~

. . . .

1. Preheat oven to 350°F.

2. Spread sweetened coconut on a baking tray and bake for 7 to 10 minutes, until lightly golden. You might want to ask an adult to help you take the tray out of the oven. Let the coconut flakes cool.

3. Put the butter and powdered sugar into a bowl, and using a handheld mixer, cream together until smooth and light. Make sure your butter is really soft, and go slowly at first; otherwise, you will have powdered sugar flying about all over the place! Mix in the vanilla extract and coconut milk, slowly adding more coconut milk until a

lovely creamy texture is reached. Dip in a clean spoon and give it a taste.

4. Swirl on top of cooled cupcakes.
5. Sprinkle the toasted coconut flakes on top.
6. If there are any cupcakes left, store in an airtight container at room temperature.

Chocolate Butter Bread

Makes 1 Bundt cake

Marie Claire makes this only on Wednesdays, because in her experience Wednesdays are often days when people need something special to eat. One buttery, chocolaty mouthful, and the gloomiest Wednesday will be transformed by happy smiles.

This is a little bit more complicated than the other recipes but worth trying because it is simply so delicious. It is definitely best eaten warm from the oven!

~ INGREDIENTS ~

2 teaspoons dried yeast

3 cups all-purpose flour (plus about another ¼ to ½ cup)

¼ cup sugar

⅔ cup lukewarm milk (Just warm in a microwave for about twenty seconds, but be careful because you want the milk only slightly warm and not hot.)

½ teaspoon salt

½ cup (1 stick) butter

2 large eggs

1½ teaspoons vanilla extract

5½ to 6 ounces of good dark chocolate (The better the
   chocolate you use, the more delicious your bread will
   taste. Marie Claire is a big fan of Callebaut and Lindt.)

~ METHOD ~

. . . .

1. In a small bowl, mix together the yeast, ½ cup of the
    flour, the sugar, and the lukewarm milk. Let this mixture
    sit for about 10 minutes, until it gets all foamy and
    bubbly.

2. While you are waiting for the yeast mixture to bubble
    up, take a large bowl, or if your home has one, the bowl
    of a standing mixer. Most standing mixers come with
    dough hook attachments, and this is the easiest way to
    make chocolate butter bread. If you don't have a standing
    mixer, don't worry; you can knead the dough by hand. It
    just takes a bit longer, but it's also quite fun. So, into your
    big bowl put 2½ cups flour and ½ teaspoon salt. Chop
    in one stick of butter, cutting the butter into smallish
    pieces. Then using your fingers, rub the butter into the
    flour until it looks like bread crumbs and there are no big
    clumps of butter left.

3. Now add 2 eggs, the vanilla, and the small bowl of
    bubbly yeast mixture. If you are using a standing mixer

with a dough hook, gently mix the ingredients around at low speed. If you are using a regular bowl, stir the ingredients together with a wooden spoon. What you are aiming for is a soft but not sticky dough. If your dough is very sticky, take the remaining ¼ cup of flour and slowly shake some of it into the bowl, mixing it around until the dough no longer sticks to the bottom and sides. You may need a bit more, but add slowly.

4. Keep the standing mixer running for about three minutes while it kneads the dough. To do this part by hand, simply tip the dough onto a clean, floured table. Using the heel of your hands, push the dough forward, then fold it back over and push forward again. This is called kneading, and it can be quite hard work. Keep going, turning the ball of dough, pushing it forward, and folding it over again and again for about three minutes. You don't want to overwork this dough. Too much kneading will make the bread tough.

5. Put the dough into a clean bowl. Cover the bowl with a dry dishcloth or a piece of plastic wrap, and leave it to rise in a warm place. The kitchen counter is usually good. Now you need to wait until your dough is double its size. This can take anywhere from 1½ to 4 hours, so just forget it's there and go off and do something fun. You don't have to hang around the house while it's rising.

6. Chop up the dark chocolate on a chopping board that

HAS NOT been used to chop onions (otherwise, your bread will taste oniony). Try not to eat all the chocolate while you are waiting for your dough to rise. Once the dough has puffed up to double its original size, punch it down and stir in the chocolate. Use your hands for this. It's much easier than trying to mix the dough with a spoon.

7. Butter around the inside of a pretty 7- or 8-cup Bundt cake pan. Pat the dough into a circle the width of the pan, and using your fingers, make a hole in the middle so it looks a bit like a giant, flattish doughnut. Carefully lower the dough ring into the cake pan, enlarging the hole if necessary so that it fits over the tube in the center of the pan. Now cover with plastic wrap or a dishcloth, and leave it to rise in a warm place until it has doubled in size again. This should take about 1 to 1½ hours, but don't worry if it takes longer. Time doesn't matter here. Making sure it rises properly is what's important. It should rise almost to the top of the pan.

8. Preheat the oven to 375°F. When your dough has risen, bake it in the middle of the oven for 35 to 40 minutes. Check the bread after about 20 minutes. If it looks like it's getting too brown on top, cover the pan loosely with foil. As it bakes, your house will smell fabulous, just like Marie Claire's bakery. You can tell the bread is done because it will be a lovely golden color on top and sound

hollow inside when you tap it. Ask an adult to help you take the pan out of the oven and place it on a wire rack. Loosen the edges with a kitchen knife and then turn it out of the pan to cool. If you want to add a fancy touch, feel free to sprinkle some confectioners' sugar on top of the bread, when it has cooled.

9. Try to wait a bit before cutting off a slice. This is almost impossible to do, and even though Marie Claire lets her bread cool down before slicing into it, Poppy always has a big, steaming piece, warm and chocolate speckled, with her morning caffe latte.

10. Store in an airtight container at room temperature.

Charlie's Favorite Lemon Bars

Makes about 20 2-inch bars

Whenever Poppy makes these, Charlie will share a bag of them with her goose. He loves the crumbly cookie crust, while Charlie adores the zingy lemon filling.

~ INGREDIENTS FOR THE CRUST ~

(You will need to bake these in a 9 x 13 pan*)

. . . .

1¾ cups flour

¼ cup cornstarch

½ cup confectioners' sugar

¼ teaspoon salt

1 cup (2 sticks) butter

*If you want to make a smaller quantity of lemon bars, simply halve all the ingredients for the crust and filling and bake in an 8 x 8 pan. You may need to ask an adult to help you work out the math for this! The most difficult measurement to halve is 1¾ cups of flour. Half of this would be ¾ cup plus 2 tablespoons of flour.

~ Ingredients for the Filling ~

. . . .

4 large eggs

2 tablespoons finely grated lemon rind

⅔ cup lemon juice (You will probably need four to five
lemons, depending on how juicy they are.)

1½ cups sugar

¼ cup flour

⅛ teaspoon salt

~ Method ~

. . . .

1. The easiest way to make the crust is in a food processor.
   If you have one in your house, ask an adult to set it up
   for you, then simply put in all the crust ingredients and
   whiz together until a smooth dough forms. If you don't
   have a food processor, don't worry. Simply put the flour,
   cornstarch, confectioners' sugar, and salt into a big bowl.
   Stir around with a fork to blend. Chop the cold butter
   up into small pieces and tip it in. Then using your thumb
   and fingers, rub the butter into the flour mixture until it
   resembles fine crumbs. When you reach this point, squish
   it all together until it forms a soft dough. Taste a little to
   make sure it's yummy.

2. Now press the dough into your pan. Try to make the layer as even as possible.

3. Put the pan in the fridge to chill for 30 minutes before baking. This step is important. It will give you a crisper, flakier cookie crust.

While the crust is chilling, you can make the filling.

4. Crack the eggs into a bowl. (You don't want bits of shell in the filling, so you might want to ask an adult to help you with this part.) Beat the eggs with a whisk, and then add the rest of the filling ingredients. This makes a very lemony bar, which Charlie loves.

5. Preheat the oven to 350°F.

6. Once the crust has chilled for half an hour, bake it in the oven (without the filling) for 20 minutes. Don't take the pan out, but turn the oven temperature down to 300°F. Bake the crust for another five to ten minutes, until it's a nice pale golden color.

7. Now ask an adult to help you take the pan out of the oven and let it cool for two or three minutes on a wire rack before pouring on your topping. You do want the crust to be warm when the filling goes on.

8. Carefully pour the lemony filling all over the cookie crust. Then ask an adult to help you put the pan back in the oven.

9. Bake for 25 to 30 minutes at 300 degrees, until filling is set. The filling should not be liquid in the center, but a soft jiggle is okay.

10. Cool completely in the pan on a wire rack. This is hard to do, and Charlie has been known to eat the bars, warm and crumbly, straight from the oven!

11. Sift powdered sugar on top and then cut into bars and eat.

12. These are best eaten the day they are made, but are still delicious when a few days old. Store in an airtight container at room temperature.

Coffee Cupcakes

Poppy dreamed up these delicious cupcakes after drinking her first cup of French-brewed coffee at Marie Claire's bakery. This makes a rich, espresso cupcake topped with coffee buttercream and a coffee-flavored chocolate bean on top.

~ Ingredients ~

. . . .

1 tablespoon milk

1 tablespoon instant espresso powder (found in the coffee
   aisle of most supermarkets)

½ cup (1 stick) butter, softened

½ cup sugar

2 large eggs

1 teaspoon vanilla extract

¾ cup plus 2 tablespoons self-rising flour (or all-purpose
   flour mixed with 1¼ teaspoons baking powder)

¼ teaspoon salt

~ Method ~

· ·

1. Preheat the oven to 350°F.

2. Pour the tablespoon of milk into a little dish (a small china ramekin is ideal), and warm it in the microwave for about 10 seconds. If you don't have a microwave, just warm some milk gently in a saucepan and measure out 1 tablespoon into a little dish. Then sprinkle the espresso powder over the milk and stir to blend.

3. If there is a food processor in your home, ask an adult to help you set it up, then whiz all the cake ingredients together, including the espresso-flavored milk. Then go directly to step 7.

4. Otherwise, put your stick of softened butter into a large bowl, and using a handheld mixer, whiz the butter around until it is nice and fluffy. Pour the sugar on top, and beat together with the butter until well blended. Go slowly at first, because you don't want sugar flying all over the counter.

5. Add the eggs one at a time, beating well after each addition. You can ask an adult to help you with this if you like, because you don't want bits of eggshell in the batter. Add the vanilla extract, then the self-rising flour (or all-purpose flour and baking powder) and ¼ teaspoon salt and mix quickly again. You don't want to overmix the ingredients or your cakes will be tough.

6. Now mix the powerful espresso-flavored milk into your cake batter, scraping around the little dish to make sure you get it all in. The batter will turn a rich coffee color and smell delicious.

7. Arrange 12 paper cupcake wrappers inside a muffin tin, or if you want to make miniature cupcakes, you will need about 36 mini paper wrappers for a mini muffin pan. Fill each cup half full with cake batter and bake 16 to 20 minutes for regular cupcakes, or 9 to 14 minutes for minis. You might want to ask an adult to help you get the cupcakes into and out of the oven. Let cool on a wire rack.

8. Frost with Coffee Frosting when cool.

Coffee Frosting

You can make this while the cupcakes are baking.

~ INGREDIENTS ~

2½ tablespoons milk

1½ teaspoons espresso powder

½ cup (1 stick) butter, softened

1¼ cups confectioners' sugar

~ METHOD ~

1. Pour the milk into a little dish. Warm the milk in the microwave for about 10 seconds, and sprinkle the espresso powder on top. Stir to blend.

2. Put the softened butter into a large bowl and shake the confectioners' sugar over it. Using a big wooden spoon or a handheld mixer (I like to use a handheld mixer because it makes the frosting really smooth and creamy), gently stir the espresso-flavored milk into the mixture, and blend together until soft and creamy. Go slowly to begin with; otherwise, you will have sugar all over your

counter! If you want a softer frosting, just add a drop or two more milk.

3. Using a dinner knife, smooth the frosting on top of the cupcakes, and decorate with a coffee-flavored chocolate bean.

4. These are so scrumptious you probably won't have any left. If you do, store them in an airtight container at room temperature.

A Really Delicious Orange Cake

Makes 1 loaf

This is an excellent teatime cake. It is moist and orangey, with a lovely orange icing drizzled on top. It's a favorite with the villagers of Potts Bottom, and unlike Mrs. Pendle's version, it doesn't contain any canned salmon!

~ INGREDIENTS ~

1 large organic orange

¾ cup (1½ sticks) butter, softened

¾ cup sugar

3 large eggs

¼ cup apricot jam

1⅓ cups self-rising flour (or all-purpose flour mixed with 2 teaspoons baking powder)

¼ teaspoon salt

~ METHOD ~

. . . .

1. Preheat the oven to 350°F.

2. Using a lemon zester, grate the rind off the orange. If you don't have a lemon zester, you can use the small holes of a cheese grater to grate off the orange rind. Squeeze out 5 tablespoons of the orange's juice.

3. The easiest way to make this cake is to whiz all the ingredients together in a food processor. Ask an adult to help you with this if you decide to use one. Then go directly to step 8.

4. Otherwise, put the butter and sugar into a large bowl, and using a handheld mixer, blend them together until light and fluffy. (This is called creaming.)

5. Add the eggs one at a time, mixing well after each addition.

6. Mix in the grated orange rind and apricot jam.

7. Carefully stir in the self-rising flour (or all-purpose flour and baking powder if using it) and salt. Don't overmix if you can help it, because overmixing will make your cake tough. Now add the 5 tablespoons of fresh orange juice.

8. Butter a 6- to 8-cup loaf pan, and pour in the cake mixture.

9. You might want to ask an adult to help you take the cake in and out of the oven. Bake for about 40 minutes, or until light golden and the top feels spongy when you

press it. If you poke a sharp knife into the center, it should come out clean. Check after about 30 minutes. If the top is browning too much before the cake is cooked through, cover it with a piece of foil.

10. Let the cake cool in the pan on a wire rack for a few minutes. Then run a knife around the inside edges of the pan to loosen the cake, and bravely turn it out. Don't worry if some bits of cake have stuck to the bottom of the pan. They are delicious to eat, or you can scrape them off and put them back on top of the cake. Cool the cake completely before drizzling over the frosting.

Orange Drizzle Frosting

½ cup confectioners' sugar

1½ tablespoons fresh-squeezed orange juice (You should
have enough left over from the orange you squeezed for
the cake.)

~ METHOD ~

1. Put the confectioners' sugar into a small bowl and slowly
stir in the orange juice. Add a little bit at a time until you
get the desired drizzle consistency. You are not after a
thick, gooey frosting here, but a tasty orange drizzle.
Pour over the cooled cake and let set.

2. Store any leftovers in an airtight container at room
temperature. Poppy has been known to enjoy a slice of
orange cake for breakfast!

Mrs. Plunket's Rainy Day Brownies

Makes about 12 2-inch squares

This recipe was given to Poppy by PC Plunket's mother. One taste and Poppy was smitten. These are the easiest brownies in the world to make, and the most delicious. Like Mrs. Plunket, Poppy makes them only on rainy days, and they are a favorite with the Ruthersfield girls.

The ingredients listed below make enough for an 8 × 8 pan, but Mrs. Plunket always doubles the recipe to fill a 9 × 13 pan. If you like brownies, this is an excellent idea. PC Plunket has been known to polish off an entire batch in one evening!

~ INGREDIENTS ~

½ cup (1 stick) butter

2½ ounces unsweetened chocolate

1 cup sugar

½ cup flour

1 teaspoon baking powder

1 tablespoon cocoa powder

½ teaspoon espresso powder

¼ teaspoon salt

1 teaspoon vanilla extract

2 large eggs

~ METHOD ~

. . . .

1. Preheat the oven to 350°F.

2. Put the butter and chocolate into a bowl and melt
    together in the microwave. This will probably take about
    1½ minutes. If you don't have a microwave, balance the
    bowl on top of a saucepan of simmering water to melt
    (like a double boiler). Ask an adult to help you with this.

3. Once the chocolate and butter have melted, stir them
    together to blend. A wire whisk works well for this, or a
    big wooden spoon. Then add the rest of the ingredients,
    one at a time, cracking the eggs in last. Mix everything
    together well.

4. Scrape the mixture into a greased 8 × 8 square pan.
    Rubber spatulas are great for this. Cook for 25 to 35
    minutes. Check after 25 minutes. You do not want to
    overcook these. A little squidge in the middle is a good
    thing. If you like your brownies cakey, keep them in a

little longer. You might want to ask an adult to help you take the pan out of the oven.

5. Let the brownies cool in the pan on a wire rack, and try not to burn your mouth in your eagerness to eat them!

6. There are never any leftover brownies at the bakery or at the Plunkets' house. If you are lucky enough to have some, store them in an airtight container at room temperature.

Marie Claire's Little Warm Almond Cakes

Makes about 24 little almond cakes

This was the first thing Poppy ever ate. Moist, light, and almond scented, they are a small taste of heaven. Marie Claire always cooks these in a special shell-shaped pan called a madeleine pan. It makes the little cakes look really pretty when you turn them out. If you don't have a madeleine pan, don't worry; a mini cupcake pan will work just as well, and the cakes will taste delicious even if they don't look quite as beautiful.

~ INGREDIENTS ~

½ cup (1 stick) butter

7 ounces almond paste

¼ cup sugar

3 large eggs

1 teaspoon vanilla extract

½ cup all-purpose flour

¼ teaspoon salt

½ teaspoon baking powder

~ METHOD ~

. . . .

1. Preheat the oven to 350°F.

2. Butter your madeleine pan or mini cupcake pan well and sprinkle the inside with flour. Turn the pan over and tap out any extra flour over the sink.

3. Melt your butter in a little dish in the microwave. You can also do this in a little saucepan on the stove, but the microwave is easiest. It should take 45 seconds to 1 minute. Put the butter aside to cool.

4. You can make this batter in the bowl of a standing mixer (ask an adult to set this up for you) or with a handheld mixer. Beat the almond paste and sugar together. Do this slowly so bits of almond paste don't go spattering out all over the counter. It may still look sort of pebbly, but don't worry about this; when you add the eggs, it will smooth out.

5. Now add your eggs one at a time, beating well after each addition.

6. Stir in the vanilla extract.

7. In a small bowl, stir together the flour, salt, and baking powder with a fork. Then gently stir this flour mixture into the batter.

8. Now stir in the melted butter.

9. You can let the batter rest in the fridge for a bit, or use it right away. The cakes will hold their shape better if

you let the batter chill for an hour (or overnight if you prefer).

10. Spoon batter into each mold. If you are using a madeleine pan, heap the mixture up in the middle so the cakes will have a rounded hump.

11. Bake in the oven for 12 to 15 minutes, or until spongy to the touch and very lightly golden. You might want to ask an adult to help you take the pans out.

12. Cool the cakes in their pans for a few minutes on a wire rack. Then slide a knife around each cake to loosen it, and gently lift them out. Cool completely on the wire rack.

13. Now shut your eyes, take a bite, and wonderful memories will come flooding back!

14. Store the little almond cakes in an airtight container at room temperature.

~ ACKNOWLEDGMENTS ~

First of all, a huge thank-you to my amazing agent, Ann Tobias, for all her help and hard work on this book. She guided me through countless rounds of revision, teaching me the fine art of the edit, and never stopped believing in Poppy Pendle.

To Paula Wiseman, my wonderful editor at Simon & Schuster, who embraced Poppy with open arms and gave her the perfect home.

Thank you so much to Jane Gilbert Keith for all her fabulous suggestions and advice. She read this manuscript almost as many times as my mother did and never once complained.

Thank you to Bette Schmitt for giving Poppy her librarian's seal of approval and sharing her with some of the kids at Deerfield Elementary School.

I am so grateful to Janet Street, who inspired me to start writing again and gave me the confidence to believe I was good enough. And to Midge and Michael Beneville, who told me this would happen from the very beginning. My heartfelt thanks to Rachel Hass, Nancy Charboneau, Kim Rosner, Pauline Boyce, and Annabelle Fenwick, who read early drafts of this manuscript and kept cheering me on. To Annalie Gilbert

Keith, who has shown me that you only need to touch one reader to make a difference, and for dressing up as Poppy Pendle on Halloween before I even had a publisher!

For the daily phone calls and friendship, I could never have made it through without Sarah Murray. And to Rachel Roberts, who tasted and tested all my recipes with me, helping to fine-tune the perfect caramel cookie! I also need to thank Stacie Chapley, MaryLou Rosner, Micah and Lily Roberts, and Martha Price, who all kindly tested recipes from Poppy's bakery.

To my parents, for their never-ending support and for reading countless versions of *Poppy*, especially my mother, who has been my spell-checker and grammar editor ever since I wrote my first story back in kindergarten!

Last, but most important of all, a special thank-you to my family. To my four wonderful children, Sebastian, Oliver, Ben, and Juliette, who have spent many evenings patiently waiting for dinner to appear while their mother tapped away on her laptop. You inspire and amaze me every single day and I am so proud of you all. And to Jon, my biggest supporter and love of my life, who knew this would happen long before I ever did!